RELUCTANT LUMBERJACK

AN MMF STANDALONE NOVEL

LYNN BURKE

RELUCTANT LUMBERJACK

Twenty years ago, I loved a woman.

Twenty years ago, I also loved a man.

And twenty years ago, rather than choose, I abandoned them both.

Now, I'm living a lonely life, luckless in love and unwilling to confront the truth of what I left behind.

When my brother passes, I become responsible for my four-year-old niece. Uprooting her isn't an option which means heading back to the sticks of New Hampshire, to the small town I fled.

Because of Charlotte.

Because of Liam.

My two best friends, the ones I'd been reluctant to pursue but couldn't deny.

Attempting to avoid facing my past doesn't work, and I see them both—together. They appear to have moved on while I can't.

I still want her.

I still want him.

But secrets lay between us, betrayals that threaten to crack the egg shells we walk on.

I've got more than my own heart to look out for now, and I'll protect those I love this time around.

No matter the cost.

NATHAN

I washed the paint off my hands and bent a bit to check my face and beard for splatters in the small mirror above the mater bathroom's sink. Blakely had hired me to paint her bedroom and install crown molding, and after two days of chatting with her, I was ready to take my shot.

Blakely reminded me of the girl with gorgeous tits and an ass to die for I'd left behind back in the sticks of New Hampshire almost twenty years earlier. Charlotte Mathis. The memory of her curves still haunted me to the point I still wasn't looking for anything long term, nothing more than a place to park my dick until we both grew bored with one another.

I'd taken Char's virginity at eighteen because it's

what she'd wanted—and I needed to show my best friend she was beautiful regardless of her size which she'd always complained about. Who she was, every part of her, made me hard as a rock.

Because, fuck did she ever.

Thinking about Char always brought back memories of him too. Liam Headley. My other best friend and the only man I dreamed about. Even after all those years, I could still recall how his strawberry-flavored lip gloss lingered on my tongue, how he'd felt under my hands. The noises he'd made when I'd given him what he'd wanted.

I'd been both their firsts without the other knowing—and they'd stolen my heart.

Eyeing my scruffy face in the mirror, I told myself a lovely single mom—Blakely—sat out in the living room and the past was best left in the past.

If only I could convince my inner self as easily as my brain.

Loving two people had split me in two. I hadn't been able to choose between my two best friends— and I'd taken the cowardly way out, using my scholarship to play football at URI as an excuse to escape because my head and my heart refused to be swayed toward one or the other. But because of those two, I hadn't been in the game for anything permanent since blowing out my knee my junior year and ruining my chances to play in the NFL.

Yeah, Blakely had a son, and she loved him the same way my mom had loved me before she left. I saw him as baggage, and that would usually turn me off when it came to women, but she had the curves a six-foot-five, two-eighty bear like me could enjoy without fear of hurting her.

I could handle the fact she had a son until we went our separate ways. Besides, he was old enough that he wouldn't be hanging on her hip or getting in the way if she wanted a little adult time—which I hoped to get with her tonight.

Finally washed up, I turned off the faucet. Murmuring came from outside the bedroom while I dried my hands. Last I'd known, Blakely's son wasn't home, and I definitely heard more than one voice.

I picked up my bucket with the painting tools packed away and walked through her bedroom, eyeing the bed. My dick twitched at the thought of being buried balls deep inside her lush body.

A man could hope.

Ready to push for that date I'd been thinking about since meeting Blakely two days earlier, I sauntered into the kitchen—and pulled up short in the doorway my head barely fit beneath.

Some pretty boy douchebag had his arm around Blakely as they stood just inside the front door. "Are you sure you don't mind?"

I must have made some noise because he glanced my way. "Who's that?" he asked, pointing at me with his chin.

Blakely turned toward me, and same as when I'd first shown up and got an eyeful, her gorgeous smile sent a shot of lust straight to my dick even as my heart ached for the similar woman I'd left behind. "That's Nathan, the handyman, the one Carissa recommended."

The pretty prick holding her asked something about why I'd come from her bedroom, and the jealousy in his tone had me grinning, puffing out my chest a bit.

That's right, fucker. You've got competition.

"I locked him up in my bedroom the past two days." Blakely played him good too, snickering at her own explanation. The guy scowled, and she lightly touched his chest as though attempting to calm him down. "He's doing some work for me."

My grin stayed in place as his forehead remained furrowed.

"Nathan," Blakely said, "this is Stewart. He's…a friend from college."

Stewart held onto her hip with a possessive hold that suggested he was more than a mere friend.

I switched my bucket to my free hand and extended the other, forcing him to let go of her.

Stewart released Blakely like I'd wanted and shook my hand with a decent grip, but nothing compared to my bear-like paw roughened from years working as a carpenter. "What exactly are you fixing in her bedroom?" he asked.

Blakely answered before I could, explaining the color change and decorative molding, and Stewart whined about her not asking him to do the work. She reminded him he'd been in Nevada, but of course, he'd moved back home and could take care of whatever wasn't done. Or so he claimed.

From the memory of his soft palm, I doubted he could do the molding I planned to install tomorrow.

That mega-watt smile of Blakely's turned my way, refreshing my memory of why I wanted the woman beneath me. "So, tomorrow morning then?"

Guess she thought the same about her pretty *friend.*

Smirking, I glanced between them, silently telling Stewart he'd have to do more than act like a little bitch to get between Blakely's thighs. He might have his hand on her waist again, but I'd be back.

"Looking forward to it," I promised her.

Five minutes later, I sat in a bit of traffic, my smirk long faded while I replayed our conversation since leaving. Who the fuck was he, and where would he be living now that he'd returned from Nevada? Needing fucking answers, I called my friend Carissa who had referred me to Blakely for the job.

"So what's the deal with Blakely and that Stewart guy who went to college with her?" I asked the second the call went through.

"Well, hello to you too. Why are you asking?"

I inched my old truck along, following the Mercedes in front of me. "Because she's hot as hell, and I'm itching for something new."

"Bored?" she asked with a light laugh, knowing me too damn well.

"Just saw her for the first time two days ago and felt sure she's what I need in my life right now." I tugged on my beard as we came to a standstill again, pushing aside thoughts that I might only want Blakely because of who she reminded me of.

"I'll be honest with you." Carissa's tone furrowed my brow. "I spoke with Stewart earlier—"

"Wait. You *know* the prick?"

"I've known him for years. We grew up together."

"Of course you did," I muttered, cursing the pretty boy again in my head.

"*Anyway,*" she continued, "while I hate to say you don't have a chance, you really don't have a chance, Nathan. Stewart's a doctor. Blakely's a nurse. They're a good match, never mind that they're both hot for each other."

"Well, fuck."

"There's plenty of fish in the sea." Carissa's voice suggested pity more than encouragement.

I let out an exasperated heavy exhale, remembering how she hadn't shied away from the pretty boy's grasp on her hip telling me the truth.

I *didn't* stand a chance.

But at least I still had the job and would see her in the morning. Stewart might end up having her, but that wouldn't stop me from enjoying the sight of Blakely's curves and the thoughts of *what if* the prick had stayed in Nevada.

He answered Blakely's door the next morning. "John—how's it hanging?"

I wanted to smash the pearly-white grin off his damn face, and after I glanced down to find him all but naked with a towel around his hips, my hand not clutching my bucket of tools fisted.

"The name is Nathan," I reminded him even though I knew the fucker got my name wrong on purpose. "Where's Blakely?"

Still grinning, he reached up to hang from the doorframe. Just slightly shorter than me, he didn't have far to stretch. He flexed, and I barely held in my snort. Fucker didn't have anything on me—except for a lot less chest hair.

"She's…indisposed."

I lifted an eyebrow and waited.

With that fucking smirk still on his face, he let me know he was moving in with her and that *they* wouldn't be needing my services anymore since he could finish up the job. After he mentioned they would have called earlier but ended up sleeping in because they'd been up half the night, I got the hint.

"You know how it is when the love of your life takes you back," Stewart said.

I wished I could say that I did, considering the happy glow on his fucking face.

"Mail the bill, and we'll take care of it." Stewart shut the door on me before I could argue.

Scowling, I climbed in my truck and called Blakely's cell before driving off. It went straight to voicemail, so I left a message telling her what Stewart had said about not needing my services anymore and asked her to call me if I'd been misinformed.

What sucked was I didn't have another job lined up until the following week. It also sucked I'd be out of some cash, but I had enough in my meager savings to pay that month's bills.

I went back home to my tiny, one-room apartment and used my old weight bench to beat my body down.

Blakely never called.

But two days later while I tried to rustle up some work to finish out the week, a lawyer from New Hampshire rang me.

"Your brother passed," he said when I asked what he wanted.

My older brother. Dead.

First Mom abandoned me in death when I'd been five. Then Dad because he couldn't keep his drunk ass from getting behind a wheel.

I waited for regret or grief to hit while settling back in my lone kitchen chair, but neither emotion arrived, leaving me numb as usual. "What happened?" I asked, even though I couldn't give two fucks over the asshole who had abandoned me to foster care rather than take me in when our dad passed.

"OD'd."

Stupid fuck.

"He has a four-year-old daughter," the lawyer continued when I didn't respond.

Fuck. I pinched the bridge of my nose, my eyes closing. I remembered all too well the hurt of losing first one parent then the other. "And I'm his only other living relative," I muttered what I knew to be true. Why else would a fucking lawyer call me about a dead brother?

"That's correct, Mr. Oakland. Which also means all his assets—house, land, and tree business are also yours."

A hell of a lot more than I'd accomplished in my life, but that didn't make the choice easier. Knowing I didn't really have one tightened my chest and clenched my gut.

Foster care sucked ass. I'd only spent three years at the farm where the state had placed me, and even though they'd been decent people, I wouldn't wish that shit on any kid.

Especially a four-year-old little girl sick fucks would love to get their hands on.

"Where at?" I asked, dread twisting my insides.

Of course, the lawyer named the town Rawlings, the exact place where my brother and I had grown up, his house on the opposite end from where the foster farm had been.

"Give me the details," I muttered and stared unseeing at my kitchenette as my brother's lawyer explained shit to me. The legal jargon, I didn't understand, but one thing I knew for certain: My brother, while far from rich, had attained more than I had through my adult years. At least I'd been smart enough to keep off the sauce unlike our dad and steered clear from the pain pills that had caused our mom's death.

My brother had already been buried while little Trina waited in the state's care.

Glancing around my shit apartment, the truth I didn't know how to raise a kid and didn't have a role model sat like goddamn concrete in my bowels.

Baggage.

The type I couldn't bring to Rhode Island where all I did was work and survive, the kind that would take me back to a town I had no wish to visit again.

I wanted to say no to the responsibility—my brother had been a piece of shit—but Trina deserved more than I'd gotten. She deserved family to nurture her, not well-meaning strangers who didn't share blood, who could never really care, and being in the place she knew, her home, would be best.

"I'll be there in a week," I forced out, my throat thickening as we set up an appointment for me to sign some shit and meet my niece.

I wouldn't have to worry about running into Blakely and her doctor prick again—but I wondered over the two I'd left behind. Did they still live in that shithole town up in the sticks? Had Charlotte ever married and gotten those dozen kids she'd always wanted? Had Liam escaped the bullies in Rawlings, the assholes who felt men preferring dick over pussy didn't deserve to live?

Every cell in my goddamn body dragged its feet over the inevitable, but within a few days, I packed up my tiny apartment, all my belongings easily stashed in the back of my old Ford. After one last phone call to my only friends, Carissa and her husband, I set off north, my goodbyes made and a promise given to call her if I ever needed anything.

She'd been excited for my chance to start over. Something fresh and new. Maybe it would land me near a woman I wouldn't grow bored with. But I knew no one would ever compare to Charlotte or Liam. No doubt rested in my mind I'd be lonely for life.

For once, I didn't speed, my usually heavy foot keeping me at a mere sixty-five while heading north. Reluctant didn't even begin to describe my damn attitude toward the whole upheaval of my existence. And it wasn't just the idea of having a ward, being burdened with the care of a little kid. For the first time in my life, I understood what my brother had faced when our dad died—and why he'd left me to foster care.

Unwilling and yet a better man at thirty-eight, I couldn't imagine my nineteen-year-old brother's need for freedom. At least I'd gotten to live before taking on the responsibility of his kid.

I'd loved and lost by choice, a decision I continued to struggle with on a daily basis.

Hands in a tight grip on my steering wheel, I told myself that Charlotte and Liam must have moved on. Surely, I wouldn't see them in the tiny town we'd all hoped and dreamed of escaping.

Liam had always been smart as a whip and wanted to be a doctor. He'd be gone for sure, since he'd never get that kind of training up in no-man's land. And while Charlotte had planned to teach first grade, I expected she'd be married with a large brood already, her dreams of white picket fences and walk-in closets fulfilled. Regardless of what she thought about her size and crooked teeth, Char had always been sweet and beautiful enough to get any man she pursued.

I hoped for all our sakes, they'd started new lives someplace else. I didn't have the balls or emotional capacity to deal with seeing either of them living a happily ever after that didn't include me.

Because I sure as hell hadn't moved on—and I only had myself to blame.

The mile markers counted too damn quickly toward a new life I wasn't prepared for while I considered what had kept me single since leaving.

I was still in love with a woman and a man, my two best friends, the only ones who'd ever truly known me, the only ones I'd ever shared all my secrets with—except for the fact I'd slept with them both.

Piece of shit.

My scowl deepening, I let off the gas and took the exit that led to my new home, a place I didn't belong, to be caretaker to a kid I'd never met—and had zero fucking clue how to raise.

2

LIAM

I'd left Boston earlier than I'd hoped to and arrived in my old stomping grounds an hour before Charlotte expected me. Five years had passed since I'd been in Rawlings, and my stomach churned. Seeing as I had time to kill, I turned right once I got into town, deciding on the scenic route to my best friend's house for our planned dinner.

Best to meet memories head on and remind them I wasn't the scrawny, craven kid of my childhood.

After graduation, I'd moved to Boston to make a name for myself and prove my worth. Becoming a surgeon had accomplished that goal in my opinion, and I looked forward to showing the residents of my old hometown that a man like me had great value.

The middle school's ball fields opened up ahead, and I slowed. My gaze roamed over the old brick building and the side parking lot where the town bully, Billy Jenkins, had given me a black eye, I'd gotten called a faggot for the first time, and I'd met Charlotte. Even though I preferred looking at boys back in the fifth grade and had been labeled gay, the way she'd stood up to the bully, protecting the new kid without knowing me, had earned her a place in my heart.

I'd called her my newest best friend that day, and she hadn't disagreed.

We became two peas in a pod like that Gump guy said about him and his Jenny, painting our nails garish colors and sharing lip gloss.

Fatso and Faggot up in a tree became Billy and his buddies' favorite line to sing whenever they saw the two of us together, which happened to be just about every single day, but I hadn't minded. I'd dreamed about kissing boys, but I'd secretly dreamed about Charlotte in that way too. My first foster family had told me I was gay, and once they explained what that meant, I'd agreed. However, having feelings for my best friend confused me, made me question who I was. I'd learned what bisexual meant years later, but that hadn't fit since I didn't like girls. Just Charlotte.

I eventually decided I didn't need a label. I liked who I liked and wanted to kiss who I wanted to kiss, but I never let her know. She meant too much to my lonely soul to stir waters that could drown me if I caused waves.

The middle school faded in my rearview mirror, my mind fonder from memories from that time with the only girl I'd ever loved. Her dazzling smile with the crooked front teeth she hated. The tight, grounding clasp of her hand holding onto mine. The sense of belonging I felt whenever she hugged me tight.

I'd always been a needy bitch, and Charlotte seemed to know exactly *what* I needed and when.

My grin took over my face, flutters in my stomach over seeing her soon. Would she be unchanged and still beautiful? Hug me the same way even though I didn't look like I had all those years ago?

"Hell, I hope so," I mumbled to myself, rounding a bend in the road, selfishly glad she'd never married so I wouldn't have to put up with a jealous husband.

The farm appeared ahead, stirring emotion beyond what I'd expected. I slowed once more, enjoying the red and purple sunset streaking behind the massive house. Lights in the downstairs illuminated a family seated to eat dinner, same as when I'd lived there.

The state had placed me at the farm after I'd spent the first part of my childhood closer to Boston where boys like me weren't called names. But in the sticks of New Hampshire, I got shit for wearing sparkly unicorn shirts and painting my fingernails pink. In small towns, I'd learned the privacy of one's sexual orientation affected others' lives.

But how the fuck that was possible continued to baffle me.

Even though Charlotte had stood up for me, the backwoods assholes hounded me even after we got into high school. I'd been beaten up a few times for ogling boys in gym class and lied to my foster parents about how I got the bruises on my face. Too chickenshit to bring attention to myself, I'd withdrawn and studied, only hanging out with Charlotte.

Until Nathan arrived.

An angry beast of a boy who had hair on his chest at fifteen. Six feet tall, built like a man, and he shaved like a man—but was still a foster kid like me.

I'd been smitten with my roommate and trailed after him like a puppy because he let me. He never once teased me for my fag nail polish or the gloss I slathered on my lips. He never called me names, and the first time he'd stood up for me in the tenth grade ended the bullying for good.

Nathan had knocked two kids from the "kill the fag" crew onto their asses, and that day, he, too, became my best friend, joining Charlotte in my dreams and fantasies.

I drove over the covered bridge we'd fished alongside, and I smirked over memories of asking him about pussy on my seventeenth birthday. He'd had his fair share. Rumor stated he'd slept with all the sluts in school, and while he tried to explain what the inside of a woman's body felt like wrapped around his dick, I couldn't imagine touching any female like that except for Charlotte.

But she was my other best friend, and I valued her too much to mess things up just for a taste of pussy…so I'd pushed Nathan, and the recollection still embarrassed the hell out of me.

"Have you ever been with a guy?" I asked him.

Nathan studied me until I got antsy and used the excuse of reeling in my fishing line to turn away from his stare.

"I don't do dick," he stated, but not unkindly. "Have you had sex yet?"

I shook my head, too damn flustered to admit the truth out loud.

"Just be careful." Nathan cast again after his bit of advice. "Men will take advantage of you rather than take care of you. Wait for someone you trust."

"Have you..." I fought to find words while rubbing my gloss-slicked lips together. "Had a girl like that?" I sputtered over the question.

"You mean up the ass?"

My face must have turned bright red from the heat rushing to my cheeks. "Y-yes."

"Yeah," Nathan didn't hesitate to answer. "Girls seem to think sticking with anal sex keeps them virgins, but what the fuck ever. If a man isn't careful, doesn't prepare a girl—or guy—right, it can cause serious damage. Don't just give it up to the first guy wanting to stretch your hole, Liam."

MY DICK HAD THICKENED over the idea of Nathan damaging me, I remembered, and I'd almost begged him for it then and there. I'd bitten my lip and thought things through carefully over the next couple of weeks like I always did when needing to make a plan, eventually coming to one conclusion.

Nathan was the only guy I had trusted to make me a man, and a month later, I grew the balls to ask him.

He'd said no without hesitation.

Driven to get what I wanted, I listed the pros to him being my first, same as I'd done in my own brain.

Voice and entire body shaking, I'd laid it all out, even being a bastard by reminding him of what he'd said about causing damage. He let go of his reluctance because I told him he'd always been protective and wouldn't ever hurt me.

Nathan had given me what I'd asked for.

My ass clenched at the memory, and I quickly shook my head while taking a hard left into Charlotte's neighborhood. Same as always, I fought against my body's reaction every time I remembered his gentle fingers, his massive dick sinking so deep inside me I hadn't been able to breathe.

That night had opened a door to something I'd never allowed myself to hope for, and I'd lost my heart forever.

Nathan took me voluntarily a dozen more times —his instigating—and I thought for sure I'd found my forever man, the one fate had graciously put in my path in return for all the shit she'd dished out in my childhood.

But three months after starting our secret love affair, Nathan left for college to become a football star—without even saying goodbye.

Charlotte had caught my tears. My faithful friend, even though time and distance eventually physically separated us.

Setting aside thoughts of the past, I focused on the woman waiting on the front porch when I pulled into her driveway. Her bright smile, unchanged over the years, soothed away memories long best forgotten, even if they still stung like a damn hornet.

Nothing was prettier than Charlotte losing her self-consciousness over her teeth out of pure joy. Nothing felt better than being the one who put that light in her eyes either.

I hopped out of my SUV and hurried up the stoop's three stairs, throwing my arms around her, laughing and breathing in the scent of chocolate chip cookies.

"Welcome home," she whispered against my ear, and I squeezed her a bit tighter, the soft cushion of her breasts against my chest the comfort I remembered—and a turn on.

Sure, I craved dick, but my sweet Char made me want more. Soft, feminine curves. Wet heat like a glove clasped around my dick—even though I hadn't ever experienced it for myself.

"It's good to be here," I murmured against her hairline and stepped back before she caught notice of my thickening length.

"You stayed away too long—long enough I didn't expect you to ever come back."

"Well, I'm here now."

Her smile caused more butterflies to burst through my stomach. "Rumor has it you're sticking around this time. I heard we got our very own surgeon down at our so-called hospital."

"Truth. And I'm not going anywhere," I promised. "No more running off to the big city and never phoning home."

"Yeah, about that." She backhanded my arm, and we both laughed, our friendship picking up as easily as if I'd seen her yesterday, not five years ago. "Come on in. I made you cookies, but you have to eat your dinner first," she said, grabbing my hand to pull me inside.

"Chocolate chip?"

"Of course."

I followed her into her small house, a sense of

home settling over me. Cozy and cluttered, the living room on our left hadn't changed since I'd last been in town. The worn and inviting couch where we'd fallen asleep while watching movies had me longing for more of the same. She'd added another bookshelf though, and the disorderly stacks and rows caused my OCD nature to itch.

Char needed a library of her own, one with a door she could shut to contain the evidence of her disorganization.

Well-used and smelling divine as always, the kitchen lit up with bright bulbs in the old chandelier hanging above her table.

Set for two.

With a bottle of wine—cheap, I noted with a quick glance—but my sweet Char hadn't lived a life beyond Rawlings, didn't know what existed beyond the sticks. She'd stayed close to her aging parents, teaching first grade at the school I'd met her in.

We sat down to dine, and I reached across the table to take her hand. "Thank you for this," I whispered past the sudden thickness in my throat, moved beyond the emotion I usually dealt with. No one had ever accepted me like she had, and no one outside Nathan loved me like she did.

Pink fused her plump cheeks, and not just from

the heat of the oven she'd pulled the roast from. "My pleasure, Liam."

The thought of adding to her pleasure twitched need through my groin again, but I smiled and gushed over how good dinner looked instead.

3

CHARLOTTE

"Take my imagination to Boston and let me live your life the past five years," I demanded, passing Liam the bowl of potatoes I'd mashed with extra butter and half-and-half, exactly as I remembered he liked.

"All the gory details of residency or just the good ones?" His blue eyes twinkled behind his glasses, and warmth spread through me twice as much as it used to whenever Liam Headley looked my way with his strawberry-glossed lips curled up in a sassy smirk.

"The good, the bad, and the ugly," I said with a light laugh, forcing myself to glance away from his handsome face. My best friend liked men and always had. That hadn't ever stopped me from recognizing the good genes he'd inherited from whoever had given him up to the state though.

He never spoke of his birth parents, and I never asked. While we had shared most things over the years as best friends, I allowed him his secrets, and he, mine.

Like how much I'd wished every day he'd been attracted to girls rather than boys. That wish and the knowledge it would never be granted had hit hard when Liam climbed from his car earlier in all his sharp-dressed, perfectly-groomed gorgeousness.

Pushing away the butterflies hadn't come easy, but I wanted to keep Liam in my life, and that meant platonic thoughts, actions, and feelings. I prayed the latter's ease would catch up with the first two I could control.

Liam's stories took me away from Rawlings like I'd asked, and I felt his exhaustion from working unimaginable shifts. Hours on his feet in surgery, cutting into flesh and fixing humans' inner working parts.

My nose wrinkled and stomach heaved a bit at the gore, and I stared in disbelief over half the tales he shared about time spent in surgery. A bullet removal from a heart, having to pump the damn thing with his own hands…

"Enough work stories, please." I choked down my last bite of gravy-drenched roast and shook my head when he chuckled.

"Pansy." He outright laughed.

"Sicko," I shot back, unable to keep my joy over having him in my home from shining on my face. "What did you do outside of work?"

"I didn't have time for much."

"A young, virile man," I said with a snort, still smiling. "Don't lie to me."

"I was lonelier than anything."

I rolled my eyes while wiping my mouth on the rarely-used cloth napkin I'd ironed for our dinner. "Boston. Night clubs. Dancing. Gay bars. Come on. Tell me."

"No, seriously. I lost myself in books more than I did beneath a man."

I felt that sense of aloneness, using stories to escape, and my heart ached for him. "What genre?"

"Suspense, mostly." He shrugged, the pink hue of his cheeks bringing on unwanted flutters in my belly. "Maybe the occasional romance."

I hadn't ever read the type of love stories Liam doubtless would, but my e-reader sat full of the steamier sort between a man and a woman. "Romance, huh?" I asked, biting back my smirk.

"Occasionally," he repeated, shifted on his seat, and glanced away.

"Only male on male, or did you broaden your horizons in between the pages of a good book?"

The flush on Liam's cheeks deepened, and I got up to escape the desire tingling between my thighs. I retrieved the plate of cookies I'd made just how he liked them. Chocolate chunks *and* chips. "You could have visited more if you were so lonely you actually read about girl on guy action, Liam," I told him with a teasing laugh, hoping to stifle the physical need inside my body I knew would never be reciprocated.

"I'd decided when I first left that I wasn't coming back here at all."

"And yet here you are." Smiling, I settled on my chair across from him again, my heart swelling with happiness. "Why did you come back, Liam? I know our hospital couldn't have offered a better salary than one nearer to Boston."

Liam studied me long enough with his gorgeous blue eyes I got ants in my pants and scooted like a first grader in need of the bathroom. "Various reasons, but the main one being this place actually feels like home," he finally answered.

I swore he thought more, perhaps even wanted to say more, but didn't. "Well," I sounded way too breathless, "I for one, am thrilled to have my best friend back."

"Same, and as for the haters, as much as the people in this town don't appreciate my sexual preferences—"

"It's none of their damn business," I shot out, helping myself to a cookie to ease the ache of the reminder.

"—they'll appreciate having a surgeon around who knows what he's doing."

"Arrogant, much?" I asked, one of my eyebrows arching as I bit into chocolaty goodness.

"Truth. But no brag—just fact. I'm skilled with a scalpel, and this town is lucky to have me."

"They are." I decided to let him off the hook, allowing him whatever other secret reasons he had for coming home. "Now seriously, tell me about your love life and all the hearts you broke down there in the big city because I don't for one minute believe you stayed shut up in your apartment for five years only *reading* about getting laid."

"No one worth mentioning," he said with a sigh.

"But plenty of penis?"

Liam barked a laugh. "Dick, Char. Say *dick*."

"Penis," I said around a mouthful of cookie.

"How about cock?"

I shook my head, heat flushing my face over the words my mother hadn't ever allowed spoken in our home.

He continued to chuckle. My parents had been a little old-fashioned, and their teaching had stuck, regardless of Liam and Nathan's influence. "There may have been a few guys, yeah," he finally admitted.

A few, so way more than me. I grabbed another cookie rather than dwell on that depressing thought.

"I dated two different guys, but…" He shrugged.

"Neither were the one, huh?" I asked, hating the tiniest bit of happiness I felt over that fact. Liam had always been mine, and while not in the way I would have liked, I couldn't help but dream about more.

Liam shook his head, his mop of brown curls falling down over his forehead.

My fingers itched to smooth the strands back and cup his clean-shaven cheeks, but instead, I cleared my throat, pushed back from the table, and gathered up our plates. From our affectionate past, I knew Liam wouldn't pull away, but I couldn't take the chance of worsening my want for him.

"Let me help," he murmured, his voice a soothing tenor that tingled all my girly bits.

We stood alongside one another, hips sometimes brushing while I washed and he dried the dishes in companionable silence. In all the years I'd known Liam, we'd never once had a quarrel and never once encountered a problem too big for us to reason out. But then again, when you knew someone as well as Liam and I did each other, words weren't necessary.

"Would you like to go house hunting with me tomorrow since I don't have to be in the office until next Monday?"

I opened my mouth to offer my spare bedroom but quickly thought better of it. Liam enjoyed his privacy. And the thought of him bringing a date back to my house twisted my stomach up tight. "I would love to."

We took our wine to the living room, and having calmed the butterflies enough, I allowed myself to sit against his side like in the good old days, my feet tucked up beneath me. He'd traded in his teenage body spray for a spicy cologne that made me think of the city and the wild night life he'd enjoyed a time or two.

"You smell different," I grumbled, allowing myself the pleasure of quickly sticking my nose in his neck like I'd done when we were teenagers. Nothing smelled better than a man's skin. Nothing. But if he knew how the warmth of his soft skin on my nose dampened my panties, he probably would have jumped up like he did whenever a bee flew too close.

"You don't like it?" he asked as I scooted a few inches away.

"It's not *you*."

He chuckled. "Tell me about your life these past five years, Char. How come no man has snatched you up yet and given you all those babies you always wanted?"

My eyes stung and heart squeezed in my chest over his teasing, but I didn't take his question as insensitive. He didn't know all I had been through in the previous couple of years. I'd complained to him too many times I had high standards—impossible ones when it came to men. Because I'd loved two men for most of my life, and nothing on earth would ever compare to either of them.

He also didn't know I'd talked Nathan into taking my virginity on my eighteenth birthday and he never would. I'd been a horrible friend, sleeping with the one man I knew Liam had always wanted.

The same man I still dream about.

But my heart longed for Liam as well, and if he

ever found out I'd been the reason Nathan left New Hampshire, he would be angry with me.

And I would lose my best friend.

"I don't need a man," I finally stated quietly, even though I lied. If only the gods above could morph the two men into one and Cupid pricked the man's heart for me… High standards. "A woman can have babies without one, you know," I rasped, loss and longing swelling inside me.

"Is that your newest plan?" Liam asked, tugging on my long hair falling over my shoulder.

"My parents gave me the money," I blurted one of the secrets I'd kept from him.

He stilled. "Artificial insemination?"

I nodded and swallowed hard, fighting off tears I thought finished for a time. "I've tried twice with no luck. I'll learn in the next couple of weeks if this latest took. It's my final chance," I whispered, my eyes welling regardless of my determination to stay strong. "I don't have enough money for another attempt."

"Char." Liam wrapped me in his arms, his tight hold squeezing a tear out beneath my clenched eyelids. He didn't offer words of condolence or good luck but held me while I allowed a few more tears to fall. His presence encouraged me beyond all the words of my family who knew what I attempted. His arms eased some of the ache of previous failed pregnancies when others' condolences hadn't.

Either fate would allow me a baby or it wouldn't. And same as every other disappointment in my life, I would learn to traipse through the outcome. It just meant more coffee, wine, and chocolate. After years of experience, I knew I could live with that.

My first disappointment had been falling instantly in love with the curly haired, blue-eyed new kid in school, the one Billy Jenkins and his crew had teased and bullied for being gay—my second disappointment. But, my heart had fallen for Liam even though he liked boys rather than plump girls.

Two outcasts drawn together in their shared misery of not fitting in, not being normal. Him for his sexual orientation, me for my horribly crooked teeth and size. I'd always been a chunky little kid, but when hormones had kicked in, so had weight I'd never been able to successfully shed. No diets helped, and starving myself wasn't an option.

I loved my food, and unfortunately, I'd never grown enough height-wise to balance out the horizontal expansion.

Fatso and Faggot up in a tree...

I recalled the voices, but the words no longer

added to my insecurities. Like Liam, I was who I was, and if people didn't like it, they could go suck an egg. At least, I included those words as part of my daily affirmations.

The struggle remained, however, especially knowing I could never be what my needy Liam wanted.

I shared the bigger endeavor I faced, telling him of my attempts to become pregnant and the resulting heartache. How every morning when I walked into work to greet my precious students, my eyes welled with tears over possibly never sending my own child off for their first day of school. He never once whispered he was sorry while I spilled my guts, simply squeezed me tighter, his hot breath against my forehead and the warmth of hard muscle eventually registering in my brain once silence settled between us.

"So," I said, ready for a conversation change and pulling away from him before my hormones roused over something they could never have. "Movie?"

"What about the rest of your life?" He chuckled, tugging on my hair, graciously agreeing to let the topic of my life-consuming dream go. "No horror stories of school? None of those *precious* bratty first graders wetting their pants and getting laughed at?"

"My life has been a hell of a lot more boring than a hot, single surgeon's living in Boston."

"Bullshit. Tell me."

"Poopy," I muttered what my Mom always did whenever someone said that word in front of her.

"Shit, shit, shit."

Backhanding my chuckling friend, I settled in again, but not too close, and told him everything of interest I'd done outside of attempts to become pregnant in the previous five years, spilling my guts over heartache from dating app guys standing me up all the damn time to saying goodbye to my kids in the first-grade class the week before.

"Each and every one of those kids was special to me," I said, swiping at another tear sliding down my cheek. "I haven't been lucky in getting one of my own, so I give them all the love I have in my heart even though it hurts every day seeing what I can't have."

Liam placed his hand on my lower belly, his baby-blues filled with such acceptance and love he stole my breath.

I tore my focus off his glossed lips and simply held still while he caressed the layer of fat beneath his hand.

"I wish you the best, Char. I'll even pray to a god I don't believe in for your dreams to come true."

If only he knew the other kind of dreams I had— the secrets—of him as well as our long-lost friend. The man I expected we both still loved to the point it kept us from moving on.

4

NATHAN

The lawyer met me at my brother's house—a goddamn shack for lack of a better word. Moss-covered shingles, old clapboard siding in need of scraping and new paint, one busted-out window-pane duct taped over…

My gaze trailed over the stone foundation, and I made note of a decent-sized crack I hoped could be patched. The porch sagged and groaned under my weight, and I added that to the mental to-do list in tallying my brain. Unlocked, the front door pushed right into the kitchen. It fucking stank of dirty dishes and trash.

"Fucking pig," I muttered, eyeing the place as the lawyer cleared space on the small table at the room's center.

He didn't comment, but I couldn't keep from scowling at the filth on the countertops and back-splash. Even my damn shoes seemed to stick here and there on the old linoleum. Forget a handyman's dream job—my brother's place was a goddamn nightmare, and poor Trina had called the shithole home.

Maybe I'd have been better off ripping up her roots and dragging her down to Rhode Island where I at least had a couple friends. Even camping out on a sleeping bag at my old apartment would have been better than the slum where she'd spent the first four years of her life.

Too fucking late to change your mind, I told myself while I hung my overnight bag on a peg by the front door.

Sitting across from the lawyer, I focused on scribbling my signature a few times so I could get to work on creating a better environment for a little girl I didn't even know.

"Let's get this done," I muttered, the responsi-bility for Trina fully settling on my shoulders. "I've got a lot of shit to do."

No pity lined his face, just pure, emotionless business.

A half-hour later, I'd signed my name a dozen or so times and stood on the crooked, wooden stoop, watching the lawyer drive off.

Child Services, he'd said, would be by in the morning with Trina, leaving me the rest of the day to clean the place up a bit.

Two barrels sat outside the back door, and I overflowed them with the rubbish from the kitchen and rotten food in the fridge alone. I hadn't brought along much in the way of groceries, but I left my stuff out in the cooler in my truck until I bleached the hell out of my brother's outdated kitchen.

He had a variety of hardly used cleaning supplies under the sink, and the local shopping center delivered. I managed to grab the last delivery of the night and felt like a real housewife when it arrived. I stank like chemicals and air fresheners by the time the sun sank, but at least the shack sat decently clean and ready for Trina's arrival in the morning.

After I packed the delivered food in the cabinets I'd scrubbed out, I sat on the dilapidated couch and hit the power button of the TV's clicker.

Black screen.

No cable, no nothing.

Grumbling, I grabbed a beer and escaped to the

tree-encased back yard. I used an old-as-fuck axe to split a few logs by the dilapidated fire pit I would need to rebuild and eased my ass onto a rickety lawn chair. Night sounds rose around me, chirps of an occasional bird and the little frog things that cheep-cheeped from the wetlands off to the east. Stars littered the sky, and I peered upward, that soft sentiment of being a kid and laying in the hay fields of the farm rolling over me.

Liam.

My throat tightened, and I swigged my beer, forcing the cold brew down past the thickness.

We had taken our lust out to the farm's fields after our first time together. I had told Liam I didn't do dick, and I hadn't until him. I'd given him what he'd wanted, and it turned out I liked jerking him off and fucking his ass enough to push for more. Longed for it more than pussy that summer, and he willingly yielded, crying out my name every single time like a goddamn prayer while coming.

Closing my eyes against the stars overhead, I cursed myself for being an asshole, not for the first time.

He must have hated me for taking off without a goodbye, even though both he and Char had known I'd gotten a full ride to college for football. I'd headed south, leaving no forwarding address, no phone number.

Leaning forward, I propped my elbows on my knees, bottle neck dangling from one hand while I stared into the small fire shooting embers into the dark sky.

The night before I'd left, Charlotte had offered me her virginity—same as Liam had earlier in the summer. I'd accepted that gift and, like a true asshole, took off the next morning, earlier than originally planned. The feel of her beneath me had sealed my damn fate.

I loved two people and couldn't bear the thought of having to choose one over the other.

The fire crackled and popped, my only company, but my cell dinged, pulling me away from the past.

Carissa: **How'd it go?**

Lips in a thin line, I typed back with one hand. **Settled in for the most part. Meeting the baggage tomorrow.**

Carissa: **I hope she changes your mind on that.**

I doubted it.

Carissa: **Please keep in touch, Nathan. Maybe we can get up to see you later in the summer.**

My scowl eased a bit. **I'd like that.**

Carissa: **Call me if you ever need to chat.**

I expected lots of need for advice would arise in the first week of becoming a guardian. A heavy sigh sank through me—and the fucking lawn chair crunched under my weight. I tumbled to the ground, and a grunt ripped from my lips.

"Fucking piece of shit."

I picked up the mangled chair and tossed it into the night, stomping the whole way back into the shack. At least my asshole brother had an extra set of sheets in the bedroom closet. While they didn't smell like dryer sheets and home, they were clean and would get the job done.

Sleep brought dreams of hay fields, heated kisses, and muscled backsides, but Liam's mouth tasted of Char's sweetness, the heat of him clamping around my dick as tight as her body had welcomed me that one time I would never forget—or regret.

MY DAMN NERVES got the best of me come morning, and I ended up sharpening and taking the axe to the pile of wood again, hacking away to build up a stockpile for the shack's sole source of heat for the winter—a goddamn woodstove.

The downward swing and tiring effort felt damn

good. Not smashing exactly, but it got the job done of letting out aggression and stress all the same.

I didn't mind the work, and seeing as how I decided to get my brother's tree business set back into order in the next week or so, we'd have free heat and save the labor to supply it.

Oakland Tree Service employed two guys, which I'd learned earlier that morning after speaking with both over the phone. One ran the chainsaws, and the other chipped the wood and cleaned up. I told the two younger men I didn't know jack shit about felling trees but promised we'd be getting together soon—they wouldn't be losing their jobs just because my asshole brother rotted in the ground.

Both seemed relieved and looked forward to getting together.

And my insides twisted over meeting Trina.

After cleaning her room the night before, I'd prepared myself for what I would see. All her clothes were second-hand, some pieces threadbare, the socks more often than not with holes in the heels and toes. Scuffed shoes, broken toys, a flattened, old pillow, and a single chest of drawers that even I had trouble opening sat in her small bedroom.

And the state of her mattress? I'd already called

up a local store for a delivery and told them to include a waterproof pad too.

Ten a.m. arrived, and the state's people pulled up in a tan sedan. Two women in their forties or thereabouts climbed out, followed by one little girl in a faded pink dress, holding an equally faded blanket and what looked like a lamb. Wasn't too white if that's what the stuffed animal was.

She walked with hesitant steps. From sadness over the truth her daddy wouldn't be there to greet her or my size, I didn't know. I couldn't do shit about the first, so I squatted on the broken-up cobbled walkway before the women brought her too close, knowing my mass would intimidate no matter how much I tried for a smile inside my beard.

Big blue eyes peered up at me as she approached, and she popped her thumb out of her mouth. "Unca No-No?"

Fuck.

I swallowed hard, my smile wobbling over her little, innocent voice nicknaming me when I'd thought of her as baggage. "Yeah, baby girl. I'm Unca No-No," I rasped out. "Are you Trina?"

She nodded.

"What's her name?" I asked, motioning toward

the lamb with my chin, my goddamn heart aching over its dirtiness.

"Lambey."

"Of course it is. Think I can hold her for a minute? I'm feeling kind of nervous right now and could really use a hug."

Eyes all serious, plump little lips rounded, she handed me what must have been her life's treasure.

I cuddled the stuffed animal to my chest and whispered my thanks, petting my thick fingers over its filthy head. Trina watched me while I studied her pale face. Poor kid needed to put some meat on her bones. A faded bruise on her cheek had me wondering—but I couldn't think on that shit. It had to be enough knowing she'd be safe with me. Cared for. Hell, maybe even loved if she kept up with those puppy dog eyes.

"My daddy died." Trust a kid to get to the heart of a matter.

Goddamn chest seized up tight.

I kissed Lambey on the top of its head before handing it over, struggling to find words to reply to her blunt statement.

Trina snuggled the stuffed animal close and popped her thumb back in her mouth.

"My brother died," I heard myself say, and even

though I couldn't give a shit for myself, grief for the innocent in front of me rose to choke off my voice. "So maybe we can hold each other's hands while we're sad. Would that be okay?" I whispered.

She nodded, still serious and eyeing me.

I held out my hand. "Want to go show these pretty ladies your bedroom? I got it all cleaned up last night, and this morning when I looked in there to make sure everything was ready for you, I saw that all your stuffed animals in the corner moved to sit on top of your pillow, waiting to welcome you home."

She smiled around her thumb, the haunted look in her eyes fading.

"Seriously," I said, wiggling my fingers, my lips tipping upward. "Want to go see?"

Her hand slid against mine, her thumb wet from her mouth, and I closed my paw around her tiny fingers. The need to wrap her in my arms and protect her from everything and everyone kicked into instinct like a goddamn boot to my gut, stealing my breath.

My heart.

I suddenly recognized the kind of love Blakely had for her son, but I also understood the doctor prick's acceptance of what I had considered baggage.

Nothing and no one would hurt little Trina again.

I stood instead of sweeping her into my arms and probably scaring the shit out of her, but I had to bend sideways a bit to keep hold of her hand. "Come on in," I told the women, unable to keep the gruff emotion from my voice.

Both had tears in their eyes too.

5

LIAM

"I appreciate you, you know," I told Charlotte while unlocking my front door Saturday morning.

She lay her hand on the middle of my back. "I don't feel like I was much help."

I pushed in the door and stepped over the threshold of the house I'd signed papers on the day before in a quick sale. An old Victorian, recently renovated—since I had zero wish to do anything but move in and move on with my new life.

Freshly painted inside and out. Updated kitchen with all the bells and whistles, and I glanced at the six-burner gas stove, hoping to smell freshly baked cookies soon. Refinished hardwood floors led from the kitchen into the living area, all the way up the stairs with gleaming banisters toward my new master bathroom with its massive shower and jet tub.

Way more than I would ever need for myself, but I had hopes and dreams, and putting down firm roots started with a sturdy home, one that felt right.

Charlotte held my hand when the realtor had shown us the house weeks earlier, and every little sigh, every burst of light in her eyes when she'd touched surfaces like the granite countertops and the tub sent a strange dose of longing through my chest.

Yes, I loved the house with all its updates, but the sense of rightness, of belonging, had been what swayed me.

I imagined Charlotte in my kitchen pulling out those pans of chocolate chip cookies my nose longed for. I imagined watching her behind my shower's glass door, water running in rivulets down and around her lush curves.

Clearing my throat, I tossed the keys onto the kitchen island and turned toward my best friend. "Movers will be here in an hour. Want to order some pizza?"

"Sure."

"Half mushroom for you and half sausage for me?" I suggested our usual order.

Charlotte's lips quirked, but not in the full-on smile I'd come to expect. "Sounds good."

She turned away, hiding tired eyes, and meandered to the door leading onto the back patio and the fenced-in yard beyond. Her shoulders stooped a bit, her long hair swept back in a messy bun rather than flowing with its usual waves.

I sat with a heavy exhale at the island and called in our pizza order.

Charlotte continued to look over the back yard even after I hung up.

"Char."

"Hmm?" she murmured from across the room.

"What's bothering you?"

Her shoulders hitched a bit, and I waited, catching the sound of a sniffle.

I hopped up and hurried over to her, wrapping my arms around her from behind. I rested my chin on her shoulder. "Talk to me."

"I'm not pregnant."

My heart fell as a sob caught in her throat, and I squeezed her closer, my eyelids falling shut. Her final chance, she'd told me. I couldn't imagine the sense of loss, the ache in her chest she carried on her own. If only I could take half her pain…

She clasped her hands atop mine, resting on her belly. "I've never wanted anything so much in my entire life," she whispered through her tears.

I pressed my cheek against hers, not caring about the wetness smearing between our skin. "What can I do for you, Char?" I whispered past the tightness in my throat.

"There's nothing you *can* do. Sometimes fate just refuses to be swayed."

I closed my eyes and breathed in her sweet scent, focusing on her broken voice and heartache and wishing I could carry it. I tried to ignore the distracting feel of her back pressed against my entire front like a lover's embrace.

Lover.

I can give her a baby.

The thought jacked my eyes wide and kicked immediate life into my groin. I eased back, but the idea of impregnating her stayed in sharp relief in my mind, continuing to give my dick needy ideas.

"I guess I could always save up my pennies to someday adopt. I don't have energy to try this way again. Maybe I could foster until that time too," Charlotte murmured, swiping the tears from her cheeks as I put a few inches between our bodies so she wouldn't notice my hard-on. Her other hand still clutched mine at her middle. "But I really hoped for one of my own."

I swallowed hard, knowing my mouth was about to take over my brain for a change. "There are other ways."

Charlotte let out a sigh, and I longed to pull her tight against me again, allowing her to feel what I'd meant with my words. "I've tried the whole dating thing and got stood up more often than not. I even took some co-workers' advice and joined a dating app. It's just not for me. Everyone I chatted with was only looking for a hookup, not a good girl who enjoys cooking and eating too much, a woman who would love to be barefoot and pregnant in their kitchen."

Again with the shot of lust and the vision of her in my home.

I usually took my time weighing decisions, the pros and cons, and making sure a path lay clear before taking the first step in any direction, but something inside me pushed me to move forward before giving my idea full thought.

"Maybe I could give you the baby you want," I said on a rush, my throat dry and heart thumping.

"I can't afford another procedure."

"No." I tried to swallow and slow my racing heart. "I mean give you one the old-fashioned way."

Charlotte stilled, and I held my breath, my pulse pounding in my ears.

"You like men," she said.

"But I like you too," I finally admitted after years of bottling up my feelings for her. The words eased a deep part inside me I hadn't realized had been tensed up tight.

She turned, and I stepped back on shaky legs, giving us both space, preparing myself for possible rejection. Luminous dark eyes peered up at me, still freshly wet from tears, her black lashes clumped together with those unshed. "I know you like me as a friend, Liam, but this…that's a lot to offer."

Not an outright no.

A smirk lifted the corner of my mouth before I could stop it, and I clung to that lighthearted feeling since nerves wrecked my insides. "I don't have a *lot* to offer, but average can get the job done," I stated with a bit of sass while cocking one hip out to the side, hoping to sound and appear my normal, confident self.

She let out a beautiful laugh and backhanded me. "Be real."

"I am." My smile diminished as I studied her face, all sass escaping me in the seriousness of the situation. "You know I would never stand you up, Char."

The happiness on her face faded too, and I waited, my mind still racing over what I'd spilled in the most vulnerable moment of my life.

Was she disgusted? Turned off by an openly gay man offering such a thing? Her eyes didn't reveal either reaction, but I still shifted while giving her time to respond.

Her tongue flicked out to wet her lower lip, the action causing my dick to twitch. "You're serious about the liking me thing?" she asked with careful words, but her tone revealed an eagerness I hadn't expected—or hoped for.

Time to spill of one of my secrets.

I inhaled a quick, shaky breath. "Charlotte, you're the only woman who's ever given me a boner, and you have from the first day I met you," I spewed and cringed, expecting her disgust.

She blinked, her eyes widening. "Liam!"

She didn't believe me.

To hell with it.

I grabbed her hand and shoved it against my hard length—the motion caused her eyes to widen even more, and her lips parted on a quick inhale as my dick jerked in the forced hold. "I wouldn't lie to you."

Her throat worked, her gaze dropping to where I held her hand against the bulge in my jeans. She didn't squeeze, didn't feel me up, but she didn't pull away either.

"I'm offering myself, Char," I rasped out, more nervous than I'd ever been. A huge chasm of unknown lay directly in my path, opening wide to swallow me whole. "No strings, no expectations."

Tears filled her eyes again as she lifted her focus to my face, the beginning of hope blooming in her beautiful dark eyes. "And if our bodies can't create life together?"

Again, not a no.

The tension in my shoulders eased the slightest bit as another heavy exhale left my hard-working lungs. "Then we can at least say we tried."

"What if having…*sex* becomes a stumbling block in our friendship? What if it rips us apart?"

"It won't," I didn't hesitate to say, knowing my love for her, my attraction toward her would never change.

"How can you be sure?" She glanced away, and I released her hand. Charlotte wrapped her arms around her center, her eyebrows furrowed.

I stepped back again, giving her more space, even though I wanted to pull her in closer, finally taste her lips, touch her skin. Bury myself in her softness, maybe give her what she longed for.

But Charlotte didn't act like a woman interested in me as a man, and the thought she might never be open to more than a mere exchange of bodily fluids deflated my dick's focus on finally loving her the way I'd always wanted to.

A knock sounded on the front door, breaking the poignant moment and giving us space I didn't want between us.

6

CHARLOTTE

"That's probably the pizza." Liam spun and left me staring after him, and I tightened my hold on myself.

My best friend, *gay* friend, wanted me sexually. Mind officially blown, I studied him as he pulled out his wallet and paid the pizza delivery girl waiting at the door. Broad shoulders for a guy under six feet, tapered waist, a lithe swimmer-like body I'd snuggled against countless times in the weeks since he'd returned home—I wouldn't mind his suggestion one bit.

Heck, it's what I'd always wanted.

Warmth spread through my body.

Liam offered the perfect solution to my problems. A willing man. An obviously willing penis. A shudder rippled through me. Very willing. Enticingly so.

"Char?"

I jerked my focus off the bulge in his jeans, and he grinned at me while setting the pizza box on the island. "Hungry?"

Oh boy.

My smile wobbled, and I forced myself to release my arms and move toward him. "Yeah," I squeaked out, meaning more than just for pizza.

His sassy smirk widened, confidence overtaking the vulnerability in his eyes during our sex and babies conversation. "Guess I don't have to ask if you'd be up for that tumble in the sack, huh?"

I swatted at him again, both of us buckling in laughter, mine tinged with nervousness. Either I hadn't hidden my thoughts over his suggestion or he knew me too well.

"Is that a yes?" he pushed, flipping the box's lid and releasing mushroom and sausage-scented steam.

I trusted Liam fully, and if he said sleeping together to create a baby wouldn't cause problems for our friendship, I had to believe him.

"No strings," I reminded him of his words, needing to let him know I *didn't* expect him to set aside his desire for men just for giving me his sperm.

"I won't ask for child support. I'll sign whatever legal papers you want. We can have them drawn up just like ones I signed for the artificial insemination."

He sat on an island stool, his eyes once more serious while peering at me. "What if I want to be involved in the child's life?"

My breath left in a rush. I sank onto the other bar stool beside him, my legs suddenly weak. Having a child with my best friend and raising that child together would come easily with how well we got along.

"I wouldn't ever want a child between us to hold you back," I said. "From anything or any*one*."

Grinning, he turned the box sideways, creating one cardboard plate loaded with pizza and one empty—his side. "Let's eat," he said, sliding two slices from the pie and pulling them over onto his side, "and not worry over a future we haven't even tried to create yet."

"We need to discuss the details, Liam."

"Bottom line is I have sperm you need, and I'm willing to give it to you at no cost, no expectations. A simple gift."

He made it *sound* simple, but I had a feeling it would be anything but.

"Hopefully, an enjoyable one," he murmured, the

heat of his stare on the side of my face causing blood to rush to my cheeks.

Oh.

I blinked and quickly glanced down at our lunch before my eyes revealed how much I had always wanted him. How much I dreamed about a shared *enjoyable* time in bed. Shoveling the end of a pizza slice in my mouth kept me from having to reply.

THE MOVERS ARRIVED, and for the next six hours, I helped oversee the distribution of Liam's belongings he'd kept in storage near Boston. Every box and larger item, he'd labeled, making the task of getting things to their proper room a breeze.

Together, we set up his bed, one of us on either side while putting on sheets and his comforter. After that, we unwrapped his couch and rummaged through his kitchen boxes for wine glasses. He poured a bottle he'd brought from the bed and breakfast he'd lived in the previous couple of weeks.

I sat on the couch, sweaty and tired, angling toward him as he lifted his glass to clink against mine.

"I can't thank you enough," he said.

"My pleasure," I replied with a small smile.

His focus dropped to my lips as I sipped my wine. "Stay with me tonight."

A shot of adrenaline rushed through me.

Liam shifted his attention back to my eyes, and that heat simmering beneath my skin tingled my girly bits. He set his wine on the coffee table without taking a single taste and moved closer, his hand resting on my cheek.

I held my breath, unsure of what to do, what to say. Did I want him? Of course I did—I always had. But I didn't just desire a baby.

Unfortunately, that was all he offered.

No strings.

The brush of his lips across my mouth weakened my grasp on the wine glass, and I clutched it tighter, a whimper escaping me.

Another gentle sweep, a pulse of need between my thighs, and I kissed him back, earning a rumbling groan from his chest.

"So sweet," he murmured against my lips, his other hand cradling my cheek.

I opened at the flick of his tongue, my core spasming at the first touch of wet flesh stroking. Probing. Teasing. Liam Headley tasted even better than his neck smelled. Heart racing, I grasped at his shirt, still clutching the wine glass in my other hand.

He angled his head, deepening the kiss, devouring my mouth as though starved for my breath. A man didn't kiss a woman like that if he only had intentions of putting his sperm inside her. Maybe not strings-strings, but Liam definitely wanted more than to gift me the use of his penis.

"Stay with me tonight," he repeated between strokes of his tongue, his lips.

"T-tonight's not a good night. For that," I hastened to add.

Liam pulled back enough to look me in my face which had to be red. Thankfully, realization dawned in his eyes so I wouldn't have to remind him there was only one way I'd know for sure the final procedure to impregnate me hadn't worked.

My smile wobbled, and I cursed the pad inside my panties, surprisingly more upset in the moment over the fact we stopped making out than the fact I'd gotten my period the day before.

"Oh. Of course." A pained expression crossed his face, and he adjusted himself. "I'd still like you to stay," he said, searching my eyes.

He definitely wanted more.

I inhaled a shaky breath, my insides quivering

with equal parts happiness and nervousness. Friends with benefits—the best of friends, I had to believe nothing and no one could rip apart.

Arousal rose inside me to the choking point, but I hadn't shaved in almost a week, never mind the diaper-like cotton stuck to my panties. There was no way I would sleep in his bed. "I-I can't stay tonight."

A nod tumbled a long curl over his forehead, and the disappointment peering at me from behind his glasses fluttered my belly rather than making me feel bad. Brazen from the hormones still rushing through me, I set the wine aside and slid to my knees on the floor, intent on doing something I'd only dreamed about, something I had shamelessly fantasized over while touching myself.

"Char—"

I grasped his jeans and popped the button, my hands shaking like mad.

"Wh-what are you doing?" he rasped out.

Maybe I'd read him wrong… My hand paused. "Do you want me to stop?"

A hard swallow bobbed his Adam's apple. "No," he whispered.

I smiled up at him, knowing I'd shocked the hell out of him with my forwardness, and pulled down his zipper.

He sat back with a heavy exhale as I trailed my fingertips over the boxers separating me from his hot skin.

"I've always dreamed about doing this," I admitted, stroking along his hard length "but didn't think you would ever want me to."

"Oh, I've fantasized about it too," he said on a rush of air, hands fisted at his sides.

I reached in and pulled his penis out, which caused flutters in my belly and deep pulses between my thighs.

A slow hiss left him as I wrapped my hand around his thick girth. So hard. So hot. Like silken steel.

"I've never done this," I told him, my gaze riveted on the bead of moisture welling at the tip of his length. He didn't say a word, so I decided to fulfill one of my fantasies by leaning in and flicking out my tongue to taste him.

Liam let out another hiss as his salty taste burst on my taste buds, the tremor rippling over him giving me a sense of feminine power I'd only experienced once before. Heady and addictive—I longed for the feeling to remain with Liam and pushed thoughts of Nathan away.

More precum welled in its place, and I lapped at

that too, swirling my tongue over the entire head of his penis.

"You're killing me, Char."

A second rush of power, happiness, and lust swelled in my chest, and I closed my mouth over him, hiding my smile.

His fingers tangled in my hair, but he let me move at my own pace, taking him down as far as I could without gagging, loving on the smooth, swollen head at the top. Sucking on the tip, moaning over every salty smear against my tongue.

My entire body flushed, heated through, and I squeezed my thighs together, searching for friction to ease the ache inside me. I'd never expected to get such enjoyment from pleasuring a man.

"Char," he choked out my name less than two minutes in. "Oh, God. Char."

He grunted, his hips rising to meet my mouth once—twice—and he released against my tongue with a deep groan. I swallowed down the thick spurts, every pulse of his length in my mouth causing my core to thrum with need.

I licked him clean and sat back on my haunches, feeling like a damn queen. All-powerful. Desirable. And aroused beyond anything I'd felt before.

Liam sprawled on the couch, his head tipped

back, eyes at half-mast, glazed and sated. "Thought you'd never done that before," he said, his tenor voice smooth as silk and just as sexy caressing over my skin.

I shrugged, not needing to get into discussions of our past sexual relations, especially knowing he had ten or so more than mine.

He reached out and rubbed his thumb over my lower lip.

I set aside my temptation to bite the pad of his thumb and shivered as he studied my face.

"Let me take you on a date."

"I'm going with you to get groceries to stock your kitchen tomorrow afternoon," I reminded him with a shaky voice and a light laugh in an attempt to hide my consuming need for him.

"A real date," he amended, his tone and gaze serious.

My smile faded beneath the caress of his thumb, my pulse throbbing in my neck. A real date meant more than friends with benefits. It meant more than a sharing of bodily fluids—for procreation or mutual enjoyment. How much of himself was Liam willing to give up? Could I take a chance on...*us* knowing he also desired more than a woman could offer?

I'd wanted him too long to deny what he offered.

My body ached for his touch, his love in a way I hadn't felt for a man since my eighteenth birthday.

Recognizing my chance to move forward, I let out a steady exhale and nodded, praying my decision wouldn't end with a broken heart and torn apart friendship. "Okay."

His flashing smile lessened my unease. "Friday night. I'll pick you up at six and take you to dinner."

"I'd love that." And I hoped to love a lot more, if the promise in his eyes gave any indication of what he had planned for afterward.

7

NATHAN

Trina and I settled into somewhat of a routine. She woke crying in the night and ended up snuggled against me in my bed, hanging onto me like I was her life-sized teddy bear. More like Sasquatch-sized bear.

We sat across from one another at the table, eating toast or cereal every morning as she chatted like a magpie, telling me about her dreams, and when she asked about mine, I made up just as silly ones.

Peanut butter and jelly, her favorite meal, filled our bellies at lunch, and she still chatted, but more about her playtime that morning and the day's gossip according to Lambey.

Frozen pizzas, lasagna, and jarred sauce and pasta ended up on our plates for dinners, and after every single meal, I fought her with stern yet kind words over helping to clear the dishes. I wasn't much of a cook, but I hoped with my direction she'd grow out of her hatred of cleaning up.

I wasn't much of a playmate or hairstylist either. Trina played with the new dollhouse I'd ordered our first week together and had shipped directly to the shack while I took care of shit—both the tree business and fixing up our home. As for the hair thing, the poor kid's hung to her waist, and I ended up taking a pair of dull scissors to the tangled strands to make both our lives easier.

I stood her in front of a mirror and told her I'd never seen such a beautiful little girl. She didn't look a damn thing like me or my brother, cute and petite, and she smiled a hell of a lot more than either of us had too. But she'd put on some weight, her face a healthier color of pink since I'd landed in her life.

Her eyes glowed with happiness, and she hugged me tight, thanking me for taking away the tangles that had brought on so many damn tears I'd wanted to rip out my own fucking hair.

Unca No-No cut her hair, she told the state

workers when they came for a visit. The style had ended up uneven, but at least the strands lay clean and brushed out over her shoulders which she flounced with sass I couldn't help but smile over.

Both women had thanked me for creating a loving environment for little Trina before driving away smiling—probably over the fact they escaped her nonstop chatter.

Physically, we rolled through life just fine together, but my thoughts often lingered on those outside our bubble I had created—namely Liam and Charlotte. Staying shut up on the property, I didn't expect to hear of them or see them, which was how I'd wanted things upon deciding to return.

But a man could only be stationary for so long, even if he had a friend from his old life offering advice all hours of the day.

I had groceries and construction goods for some shack rehab sent over, meeting the two tree guys outside of the delivery people. Turned out my brother hadn't done much in the business beyond setting up the jobs, and since I didn't have a babysitter and wasn't ready to disrupt Trina's world even more with daycare, I kept business the same— thus allowing me to be home while my two guys worked the jobs I scheduled.

The stacks of cut logs they dumped on my property became my responsibility, and my new axe and I became the best of fucking friends.

Got aggravated? Split the shit out of some wood.

Stressed over Trina's whining and resulting snotty nose? Split some goddamn logs.

Got too worked up over having to use my hand to find release? Take that shit out on logs.

My muscles loved the task, my skin covered in sweat. I didn't fell trees, but I became one hell of a wood-splitter, and a single downward swipe of my axe sent firewood flying in two directions.

My brother's business had only run by word of mouth, no marketing or ads, so I kept his old cell phone as the contact number. One of the guys parked the truck and chipper on his farm, which I had no problems with. Sorting out the paperwork would take time. I doubted my brother even paid taxes, but I would get things set and running smoothly within a month or so.

The itch to move, to breathe beyond brushing out tangles, fumbling with a needle and thread to sew up stuffed animal boo-boos, and having dainty tea parties with old dolls twitched my feet.

Three weeks in, I stared down the drive toward the road, ready for a break as Trina poured our 'tea' from the cut log table I'd made for her. We sat out beneath the branches of the maple alongside the house. I needed to order groceries, but maybe it was time to head into town instead.

An older woman came into sight on the road and started up the hill of our driveway, a plate in her hand.

"Aggy!" Trina cried when she caught sight of her and left me to run down the dirt road, her hair flying in the wind behind her hurrying legs.

The older woman squatted down and hugged Trina tight, glancing my way as I stood from the stump I'd been sitting on as my chair for Trina's tea cafe.

They held hands while making their way toward me, and Aggy offered me a plate of cookies, smiling up at me.

"Welcome to the neighborhood," she said, slightly out of breath from the climb up the hill.

"Thanks."

"I'm sorry I didn't visit sooner," she said, patting at the severe bun of gray hair on the tippy top of her head, "but my knee's been giving me trouble."

"Come!" Trina tugged on her hand and led her beneath the maple tree, giving her my seat.

I went inside to grab some milk and sat cross-legged on the ground, resting against the tree trunk while Trina chatted and used her little plastic plates to hand out peanut butter cookies. Agatha poured the milk into the tiny, matching cups, and we had a real "tea" party.

She and I managed to get a few words in between Trina's excitement over having company. Widowed and alone, Agatha lived a few hundred yards through the woods to our left and had often checked on Trina and my brother, sometimes staying around if my brother needed to head out somewhere.

The way she spoke to Trina, all kindness with a soft voice, gave me a good feeling in my chest, and the way Trina loved on her and used a nickname for the older woman confirmed they had a good relationship.

"So, Agatha," I said, watching as she used a corner of her sleeve to wipe milk from Trina's chin. "You said you babysat for my brother?"

Lips pressed tight, she nodded.

I expected a lot of history lay behind the thin line of her lips, but I wasn't going to press in front of the kid.

"You're a good man, Nathan." Agatha finally gave me her attention, her eyes seeming to say more than her words.

Better than your brother.

My gaze flitted over my niece, my heart swelling with affection and that instinctive need to protect her as she murmured to Lambey, her face serious while pouring her treasure more "tea." I gave Agatha my unwavering stare. "And you seem like a good woman, Agatha. Someone I could trust to look after my little pumpkin."

"Anytime you want a break, I'm just down the hill and up the road a bit." Her lips quirked, wrinkling the skin around them. "Just not Friday nights. They're for card playing with my Gossip Girls."

Gossip Girls in small, shit town, USA—I could imagine they'd be chatting up about the Oakland boy returned home to take care of Trina.

"I was just thinking I needed to go get some groceries."

"You've been having them delivered."

I chuckled, thankful to have a watchful neighbor somewhat close by.

"My house is closer to the road than yours," she said, her eyes full of mischief, "and I just happen to sit out on my porch almost all day reading, knitting, or doing crossword puzzles. Kind of hard to miss those delivery vehicles slowing to turn up your drive."

"Sounds to me like you could use some company on occasion," I hinted with an outright nod toward Trina.

"Like I said, anytime but Friday nights." Agatha smiled.

"Busy for the next hour or so?"

Agatha picked up her tiny tea cup. "I wouldn't mind another spot of tea if Miss Trina has more?"

Giggles answered my life-saving, God-sent neighbor's question.

"Go on, Nathan," Agatha suggested. "Take a break and go get those groceries while Trina and I gossip about all the things her stuffed animals have been doing in my absence."

So I did.

My heart beat heavy in my chest as I drove into town, windows down to let in the warm early summer air. I kept the radio off and enjoyed the silence I only got once Trina fell asleep at night.

Fucking divine—but I wouldn't trade my little pumpkin for anything in the damn world. Sure, she talked up a storm worse than any nor'easter, whined more than a braying hound, and kept me awake some nights when hugging on me in bed, but she'd become my life. Gave me a reason to wake in the morning and fill my lungs. Best damn baggage a man could ask for.

But my dick had grown lonely, bored with my fist.

Getting some action would have to wait though, since I had too many other things on my plate, namely those groceries and the fact I only had an hour or so of free time. Not nearly enough to talk a woman into bedding a life-sized human bear.

My gaze flitted left to right, snagging on every dark-haired, curvy woman and every twink-like man, but I pulled into the grocery store's parking lot without having set eyes on either Charlotte or Liam.

Seeing as how I towered over most people, I drew a shit ton of attention, but I kept to myself. An older woman in the second aisle tickled my memory, and a few aisles later, I remembered she used to teach at the high school, one of the better teachers who truly cared about students. Twice, she'd sat with me after school to make sure I understood basic algebra I never used.

I backtracked, wanting to thank her for her investment in a broody foster kid, but she'd already left.

I recognized the old man bagging groceries—he'd been at it since I'd lived there before college. His watery eyes and wide smile filled me with a fond memory of ambling in with Liam and Charlotte after school some days to grab snacks before hanging out at her parents' place until dinner.

I breathed easier while wheeling the loaded cart out to my truck, adrenaline finally resting quietly even though I continued to scan my surroundings, just in case.

A shiny BMW pulled into the parking lot as I climbed into my truck, and I followed it with my eyes while buckling in. The driver maneuvered the vehicle into an empty spot closer to the store before opening his door.

Liam stepped out of the car, sunlight glinting off the rim of his glasses and the messy curls atop his head. My breath left in a grunt.

No longer a twink.

Taller than when I'd left, his shoulders wider, Liam wore a tight t-shirt that showed off lean muscle he'd always lamented not having. Prominent pecs and thicker thighs encased in form-fitting jeans.

Still hot as fuck, he swelled my dick like no other man had ever done, and I grasped my steering wheel in a death grip, my gaze riveted on his tight, round ass. Memories of owning him, selfishly taking what he offered when I knew he worshiped the ground I walked on and I wasn't gay—

Liam held out his hand, and I jerked my focus off him to find the other lover in my dreams rounding the front of his car.

Charlotte.

A groan ripped from my chest with the last bit of oxygen I had held in my lungs.

Curvier than I remembered. Her uninhibited smile lit up the goddamn world, her long hair draped over rounded shoulders and even rounder breasts that had more than filled my large hands.

A light sundress fluttered around her thick as molasses thighs, her feet in flipflops, her favorite footwear for summer.

My gaze slowly drifted upward as she turned away from me with Liam—and took his outstretched hand.

I blinked.

Stared as they walked together toward the store.

Holding hands.

They hadn't left town after all—but they both had definitely moved on. A green, ugly giant rose up inside me, and not the jolly sort who encouraged vegetable consumption like I did with Trina.

Jaw clenched, I turned the key, bringing my old truck to life, something that seemed to leech from me as Liam and Charlotte disappeared into the store —together.

While I drove home alone.

Friday morning, I couldn't contain my happiness. I had a date that night with Charlotte, and I expected she'd be in my bed when the sun rose Saturday morning.

I hoped, at least.

Having torn down the walls that hid my desire for her, sparks had erupted between us. She wanted me too, if the blow job Saturday night and the make out session on Sunday afternoon was any indication. After getting groceries, we'd devoured hot fudge sundaes with extra cherries before devouring one another's mouths.

I'd gotten my first handful of soft, feminine breasts, and even though I'd kept my touch above clothing, my mouth moving no lower than the sweet skin of her neck, I ached for more.

The scorching looks between us *promised* more after our date tonight.

Grinning, I stopped in a Dunks to get a coffee and breakfast sandwich before heading into the hospital. A rumbling engine outside drew my attention as I waited in line at the counter, and an old beat-up Chevy parked beside my BMW.

Billy Jenkins.

It'd been years since I'd seen him, but his face hadn't changed much. His massive body either, I noticed as he hopped out of his truck with a scowl on his face.

"Shit," I muttered, that gut-clenching sense of fear rising up my throat at memories of his words, his fists.

"Can I help you?"

I turned toward the young woman working the counter and forced a smile, ordering my coffee—without the sandwich since there was no way in hell I would be able to choke it down.

The glass door opened to my right, but I didn't look over. I slid my card into the chip reader and stared hard at it until it beeped its approval. After a quick tuck of the card back into my wallet, I scuttled sideways down the counter to wait for my coffee, hoping like hell he wouldn't recognize me.

"Hey, Billy," the girl said.

"Coffee," he grunted. "Black."

"You got it."

My heart pounded. Mouth dried. I stared at the shelves of donuts, refusing to look at him.

"Well, well, if it isn't little Liam the faggot boy. Heard you were back in town."

Goddamnit.

Keeping my face bland, I didn't give him the time of day.

"Regular coffee for Liam!" Another worker announced, glancing my way since I was the only other patron lingering in the store.

I nodded and took it from her outstretched hand.

Billy stuck out his elbow as I went to move past him for the exit, jostling me into a stuttered side-step. "Watch where you're going, dick sucker."

Chin high and focus on the exit, I continued to walk, my legs shaking and adrenaline rushing.

I damn near dropped my keys while fumbling to get them from my pocket, and I hit the unlock button. The second I sat on my BMW's leather seat, I locked myself in and took a deep breath.

Fucking Billy Jenkins. Asshole extraordinaire and leader of the "kill the fag" crew. He hadn't changed one damn bit, and while I had put on some weight and muscle, I knew he'd still beat me down to the ground with his height and bulk.

Longing for Nathan hit me like a bolt of lightning, swelling my throat tight and stinging my eyes. He'd had the balls to stand up to Billy, the acceptance and confidence in his masculinity to hold me while I'd cried.

I pulled out onto the main road, watching my rearview mirror—but Billy's truck stayed put.

Finishing up my paperwork, I glanced at the clock. What had started out as a shitty day had only gone downhill with two scheduled surgeries taking longer than expected, both due to complications. At least my hands had stopped shaking and both patients survived—for the time being. One lay in the ICU fighting for their life, but I'd done all I could.

I had thirty-five minutes to grab a quick shower, fly across town, and pick up Char for the date I'd been dreaming about all damn week.

Easily done, but just barely.

Butterflies swirled in my stomach, and a bounce returned to my step as I headed toward the doctor's lounge. My first smile of the day etched on my face over thoughts of a good meal, good conversation, then hopefully a good romp in my bed. Nervousness over sharing an intimate experience with a woman for the first time should have overshadowed all else, but I trusted Charlotte with my life. My heart.

Said heart thumped inside my chest to the point I wanted to jump up and click my heels together.

The overhead speaker flared to life, calling me to the emergency room, and I turned a one-eighty on autopilot, my smile fading, my steps quickening. Only one reason existed for them to request my presence there, and a fucked-up mess of bleeding bodies and sobbing people littered our small ER.

My stomach turned sour, my lips in a thin line as I evaluated the devastation.

A three-vehicle accident had left two dead, a teen with massive head trauma who required my immediate attention, and another with a crushed leg…

My mind went into planning mode, following the steps I'd been taught, movements that had become second nature. While scrubbing up for hopefully lifesaving surgery, I realized I hadn't texted Char.

She would without doubt think I'd stood her up—but it couldn't be helped.

Consumed with saving the dying teenager, I focused on the task before me, praying Char would give me the chance to explain.

9

CHARLOTTE

I stared at my cell, willing it to ring or even ding a notification of an incoming text.

Six forty-five.

Liam hadn't shown to pick me up for our date. He hadn't called, hadn't returned my text I'd shot off a half hour earlier while lingering in my foyer, waiting for him.

Stood up yet again.

My insecurities of old swelled up inside my head, and I swallowed against the tears wanting to clog my throat as the names I'd been called in childhood echoed between my ears.

Fatty Boombahlatty.

Thick Thigh Charlotte.

The fat girl no boys wanted, no one found attractive. But I'd had Liam. Until Nathan transferred to our school and I'd ended up having to share him, actually gaining another friend with my selflessness. But even Nathan had to be talked into taking what I offered, what I'd begged for on my eighteenth birthday. Sure, I'd made him hard, same as Liam the weekend before, but didn't the thought, the promise of sex, always make a man hard?

So why had Liam stood me up? He'd seemed to like my unpracticed mouth well enough, but I must've done something wrong. His rejection made my eyes sting, and I coughed to keep my throat from tightening.

Yet another disappointment in a series of failures.

I waited another five minutes, allowing myself to release my sadness before resigning myself to a glass of wine and a chocolate bar since I didn't have the makings for a hot fudge sundae. I left my spot by the front window overlooking my driveway, set aside my purse on the table inside my door, and kicked off my heeled boots.

Perhaps Liam had realized since asking me out on the date that a woman, no matter how robust, would never replace his need for thick muscle and strong hands. I expected he didn't know how to tell me, and perhaps he'd become embarrassed by the whole affair.

Eyes welling, I muttered a few curses, the sense of not being enough, or perhaps *too* much, eating at the hope I'd found in his offer of that *simple gift*.

"Stupid woman."

Blowing out a heavy exhale, I grabbed a wine glass from a cabinet, and my cell rang.

I sprinted back up the hallway toward the front door.

Mom.

The butterflies dissipated at her name on my cell's screen, and with a quick swipe, I forced a smile. "Hey." I tried for an upbeat tone.

"Guess what I just heard?"

Rolling my eyes, I headed back to the kitchen, the rush of excitement officially heartache once more. Usually, she called me *after* her Friday night of cards with the Gossip Girls over at her friend Agatha's house.

"What, Mom?" I asked anyway, yanking open the fridge door for my bottle of Riesling.

"Nathan Oakland is back in town."

My hand slipped from the handle to fall to my side, the fridge door closing back up on its own with a quiet snick. "What?" I whispered, knowing I must have heard her wrong.

"Your old friend Nathan. That Sasquatch boy you and Liam always used to be friends with. *And* he's single."

Mom's words buzzed in my ears as I stood like an ice sculpture in my kitchen, barely remembering to breathe.

My bear of a friend, Nathan.

Home. In close proximity.

No woman waiting for him in bed every night.

Heart quickening, my mind buzzed with the information.

I'd heard his brother had passed, leaving his little girl a ward of the state, but I never once considered Nathan would come back and take responsibility for a child of the man who'd turned his back on him.

"Wh-where?" I whispered, needing to know *how* close he was, but Mom kept on chatting about my crushing on Nathan back in high school and how he would surely need a good woman to warm his bed and help raise his niece. "Mom," I snipped, shutting her up. "Where is he?"

"Agatha told me he moved into his brother's place. Fixed it up right nice too. Clean and—"

"I have to go." I hit end, not caring two piles of

poop I'd just hung up on my mom for the first time since I'd been a snotty teenager.

I eyed the container of chocolate chip cookies sitting alongside my purse down the hall. They'd been meant for Liam, but perhaps Nathan and his little niece would like a housewarming gift since Liam couldn't even be bothered to text or call.

The heartache pricked again, but I focused on the butterflies in my belly. Hands and knees shaking, I grabbed my purse, the container, and my keys, refusing to think too hard or second guess my actions.

Not a minute down the road and a thought flitted through my brain. I jerked the wheel, taking me off the side of the blacktop, and slammed on the brakes, causing dust to waft past my car windows.

What if Liam had learned of Nathan's return and gone to him in a rush, completely forgetting about me?

Hands clenching my steering wheel, I bit down on the inside of my lip, tears stinging, even as my belly continued to flutter.

He doesn't know it's my fault Nathan left.

"Damnit." I stared up the road, my loyalty to Liam suggesting I turn around and allow him the chance with the man he'd loved all his life. It told me to pray he'd forgive me once Nathan explained I'd been responsible for his heartache twenty years earlier.

However, my selfishness pushed me to continue with my plan, even if just to see if I'd been stood up for a very good reason.

I decided on a drive-by, my heart in my throat and my knuckles aching from clutching my steering wheel.

I passed Agatha's house, noting all the Gossip Girls' cars still out front, and I slowed as I approached the next mailbox, craning my neck.

The long driveway up to Nathan's cabin dimmed in the distance due to the sinking sun and the plethora of trees on the property, but a floodlight off the side of the house lit the parking area out front enough I could see an old truck—but no BMW.

So Liam *had* stood me up.

Chest aching, I swallowed against my tears and turned into the driveway, pressing on the gas to take me up the hill toward the man I had loved once upon a time.

10

NATHAN

Trina had been full of spit and vinegar all damn day, first complaining about the toast I'd burned, then the sandwich with too much peanut butter I'd made for her lunch.

She whined for ice cream, so I dipped her some. The maraschino cherries had run out which caused even more tears.

She wanted to go on an adventure, so I took her out into the woods where she ended up stumbling and scraping up her knee. More crying and whining ensued while I clenched my teeth, blaming myself for not keeping better watch on the kid following in my footsteps.

After that, it was something about her stuffed animals fighting or some shit I couldn't make out past her tears. Once I got her calmed down, I put her into bed an hour earlier than usual, needing some goddamn quiet.

Trina passed out within seconds, and I realized traipsing through the woods most of the day going on that "adventure" must have worn her ass out. No wonder she'd been cranking with extra vigor from dinner time on.

While Trina had calmed, I sure as fuck hadn't. Wound tight without a pussy to lose myself in, I went out to the cut logs my guys had dropped off earlier in the day. Within minutes, I'd split a decent pile of wood and sweated enough to unbutton my thin flannel.

A flash of headlights and the following crunch of wheels on my driveway pulled my attention off the flood-lit split wood, and I swung my axe over my shoulder to keep it close by since I wasn't expecting a delivery—or company.

Scowling, I rounded the house, eyeing the compact car that slowed to a stop alongside my truck. The bright headlights glared at me, keeping me from seeing the interior.

They flicked off.

I blinked against momentary blindness, tensing over my moment of vulnerability.

The car door opened—and Charlotte Mathis came into view in all her dark-haired, curvy glory, wrapped up in tight jeans and a billowy top. Long hair brushed over the swell of her chest, and her wide hips whispered at my stunned brain to drop the axe and put my hands on her again.

Breath lost.

Dick instantly hard.

"Char," I croaked out, my goddamn feet frozen and mind fucking gone.

"Hi, Nathan," she said, lifting a container to cover her big tits I couldn't tear my focus from. "I-I hope I'm not intruding. My mom told me you moved back, and I'd just made cookies. I figured you could use a housewarming gift." The words tumbled from her mouth, breathless and rushed.

"You're not intruding," I somehow choked out past the jacked-up thump of my heart as I finally looked her full in the face. Dark eyes luminous in the light, pink staining her cheeks, her lips a berry red that caused pre-cum to ooze from my dick.

"Oh." Her smile wobbled rather than lit my world. "That's good."

We stared at one another, me backlit by the shack's porch light while she stood bathed in the floodlight spilling from my left. The last time I'd touched her rushed back to my memory in vivid detail, the sweet scent of chocolate, the satiny feel of her skin beneath my fingertips…the heat of her pussy I'd had to work my way into while kissing the soft pillow of her lips in an attempt to relax her body beneath mine.

The perfect cushion for my beastly size. Curves and softness. Wet and tight.

"Fuck." I shoved a palm back over my head, slipping the axe off my shoulder. I needed to get my goddamn dick under control.

"Are you sure I'm not intrud—"

"No," I shot out and cleared my throat. "No."

She approached with hesitant steps, and I still didn't move, too damn busy filling my eyes with the woman who'd stolen a part of my heart, the woman I'd longed for yet feared to see up close and personal again.

Swaying hips, tits heaving with a shuddered breath.

"Char," I whispered her name as she got within touching distance and stopped.

"Hi." Another wobbled smile tilted her lips up. Lips red as sin. Plump and tempting.

I fucking stared while rubbing a hand over my

bare chest. Couldn't keep from wanting, couldn't keep my insides from aching.

"Nathan?"

"Hmm?" I jerked my focus off her mouth to find her dark eyes unshuttered and honest, same as the open book she'd been when we were kids.

"Cookies?" Char held out the container, revealing tight, furled nipples poking through her blouse.

Christ. I accepted her gift, teeth clenched, attention forced back on her face.

"So," she said with a rushed exhale, wiping her hands down her thick thighs while glancing down over my bare torso. The heat of want I recognized from years past swelled her pupils. "You're back."

"Yeah." My voice rumbled from deep in my chest as I fought to get my goddamn lust under control.

"Have you seen Liam?"

Fuck, just hearing his name on those red lips had my insides all twisted up tight in a mass of confused emotions. "No," I lied rather than admitting I caught them holding hands the Sunday before.

"He just moved back too."

"Want a beer or something?" I asked, needing to be hospitable, needing to turn my back on Char before she saw the obvious bulge in my jeans and the jealousy in my eyes.

"Sure."

I spun and made for the front door, setting the axe down against the stoop. "Come on in."

The front door no longer squeaked, and I flicked on the kitchen light, glancing down the hall to Trina's bedroom door I kept cracked open. A quick peek in her bedroom showed she hadn't stirred except for her thumb to pop out of her open mouth, the somewhat white Lambey clutched close to her neck.

Quiet and peaceful—my favorite Trina.

I turned back into the kitchen, catching Char's gaze as she stood just inside the door. Her smile lit the goddamn room.

"What?" I asked, loving the flash of her imperfect teeth I remembered running my tongue over.

"That beard you've grown can't hide your crooked smirk."

My smile faded as I realized it had sprung to life over having seen my pumpkin at her best—quiet and peaceful. "You heard about my brother? His kid?"

"Yes. My mom told me."

I nodded and moved toward the fridge, my dick settled enough so I could walk without a grimace.

"I'll admit, I was surprised you took on the responsibility, considering what he did to you, but then I realized you must not have outgrown the protective nature you had as a kid."

I grunted something, not really intending for any type of response even though her assumption was spot on. She and Liam had known me better than anyone, knew most of my secrets, had held my hands when I told them about the loss of my mother, the drunkenness of my father and his demise. And the final straw to break my fifteen-year-old soul, being seen as nothing more than baggage by the only family I'd had left.

"Did you ever forgive him?"

"Fuck no." I wrenched open the fridge door, my scowl firmly in place.

"Are you staying?"

I pulled two beers from the top shelf and handed one to her, watching her gaze flit around the shack. If she'd seen the place before I'd moved in, she wouldn't be asking me that question. All the damn work I'd done to create a better home for Trina wouldn't be missed by anyone who knew what the shithole looked like before I'd arrived.

"Don't have plans to take off anytime soon," I said, giving her the truth of my future. I had no fucking clue what to do other than protect Trina until she no longer needed me.

"Will you at least say goodbye when the time comes?" She pinned me down with those dark as chocolate eyes.

"Fuck," I grumbled, rubbing at my damn chest again, unable to tell if she asked to annoy me or wanted an honest answer because she might get hurt a second time. "Want to sit down?" I motioned toward the small living room and new couch I'd had delivered.

Char inhaled, her chest rising high enough to catch my attention, but her troubled eyes kept my focus on her face. "I'm sorry for that night, Nathan. Sorry for whatever I did that made you leave without saying goodbye to me. To Liam."

I considered allowing her self-blame to continue, letting me off the hook, but what sort of friend did that? Bad enough I'd taken off and obviously hurt her—if her big, sad eyes were any indication. I expected I'd hurt Liam even worse. The kid had been in love with me since he first laid eyes on me, and when I'd given into lust and curiosity, I'd only intensified emotions—for both of us.

"It wasn't you, it was me," I finally muttered, lifting my beer for a long-assed pull of the bitter brew, hating myself once again.

Her stare caused me to shift on my feet, and I swallowed, lowering my bottle. "What?"

"That's what they all say. *It isn't you, it's me,*" she quoted with a mocking tone.

My brow furrowed. The thought of "all" those she spoke of touching her, having her, sent a rush of red heat through me, and not the lustful type. "The fuck you talking about?"

"The few men I've dated used the same lame excuse. Those that showed up, anyway." Her eyes welled, and she turned into the living room. Her booted heels clacked across the laminate then hardwood floor as she ambled toward the couch.

I followed after her like a prowling lion, ready to smash rather than pounce for a taste of her swaying ass. "Whose face do I need to rearrange?"

She sat and let out a light bit of laughter, even though it held sarcasm rather than happiness.

I stood over her, beer bottle in one hand, the other flexing at my side. "Well?"

Her gaze focused on her own beer bottle she held lightly on her lap, but she couldn't hide the pain slumping her shoulders. "I even had one guy I'd met online catch his first glimpse of me waiting for him in the restaurant. He spun on his heel after making eye contact and went back the way he came. I knew it was my date—I recognized him from his dating app picture."

Rage filled my gut, fisted my free hand at my side. "Fucker."

She drank a sip of beer and peered up at me, her eyes dark in the single lit lamp on my end table. "Are you going to stand over me and glower all night or tell me where the heck you took off to and why?"

What I wanted to do was yank her up into my arms and remind her that her curves were fucking gorgeous. All that flesh to grasp, that skin to bury my face and dick into. Twenty years, and I hadn't gotten over Char.

Not one goddamn bit.

And the desire to protect her, to be her champion hadn't faded either. She'd been a loyal friend, true and honest while I'd been a lying bastard, greedily taking what she'd laid at my feet. My Char deserved so much more than being left alone at a table for two. She deserved a man who would appreciate and love her unconditionally, accept every inch of her as a gift to be cherished.

She also deserved the truth of what I'd done.

I steeled myself to bring up the past, opened my mouth—and Trina let out a whimper.

"Be back in a minute," I grumbled, already spin-

ning on my heels to go check on my little pumpkin.
"Don't leave," I shot over my shoulder.

11

LIAM

The teen died on the operating table before I even got a real chance to save her life. While not the first patient I'd had die beneath my hand, I staggered beneath having to tell the anxious mother in the waiting room who'd been bruised up herself in the accident—and had also lost her husband who'd been driving.

I managed to keep a professional hold on my emotions while informing her of her daughter's death, but I allowed myself to grieve once back in the doctor's lounge, head in my hands, tears and snot running with abandon. The mother's wails continued to echo in my mind long after I'd delivered the news of her second tragic loss.

And it was longer still until I calmed enough to

set aside my empathy and focus on the fact *I* still lived. I still had a loved one to hold close—I hoped.

I swiped open my cell.

Char had tried calling me. Texted me.

I slowly inhaled until my lungs filled and hit dial, clenching my eyes shut and perching on the edge of one of the lounge chairs.

"Liam?" She answered, her voice quiet.

"I'm so damn sorry, Char," the words left in a rush. "I was ready to walk out the door and had an emergency here at the hospital. I didn't have time to call. I'm so sorry."

"It's okay." Her whisper sounded relieved, and I let out a heavy exhale, my shoulders relaxing for the first time in what felt like days.

"I know it's late for dinner, but can we still get together?"

I need you—need to talk to my best friend. Need to lose myself in you.

She didn't answer right away, and I popped my eyelids open.

"I-I'm not home." Her voice remained quiet, like she seemed desperate to not be overheard.

A muscle ticked in my jaw. "Who are you with?" I asked, fighting to keep my tone level over the thought she'd gone and gotten herself another date because I'd stood her up.

"Nathan."

The name registered his face in my mind, but her answer didn't fully click. "Who?"

"Nathan. He's back."

My dick nudged to life in my scrubs as my heart faltered. Talk about a damn emotional roller-coaster of a day. Like a jolt of the paddles, my pulse kicked into high gear, thrumming in my ears. "Where is he? Where are you?"

"At his brother's old house. Well, it's Nathan's now. His brother passed, and Nathan took responsibility for his niece."

Nathan's home.

And I'd just gotten back and offered myself to Char for the baby she'd always dreamed of having. I wanted that for her, but deep-seated longing for our friend fought for dominance in my head.

Emotions battled in every part of my body, wrecking me like waves against a rocky shore.

"I-I have to go," I forced out past the thickness in my chest and throat.

"Liam—"

"I'll talk to you tomorrow."

"Okay," she whispered. "Sure."

I hung up without saying goodbye, bent over, and put my head between my knees, attempting to slow my rasped breathing and the tears stinging my eyes. The scent of chemicals, of the sterile space lacking life filled my nose as I breathed deeply.

I loved them both. Wanted them both, but Nathan had skipped town, leaving me behind. Part of me hoped his disinterest remained intact because if I was forced to choose between him and Char, I didn't think I could.

The memory of the mother I'd delivered the devastating news to a half-hour earlier resurfaced in my mind. A tear slipped down my cheek.

Heartache and loss.

Severe emotional pain.

I wouldn't wish having a loved one torn from your side on anyone.

I dragged myself out of the hospital and went home to a too-quiet, too-empty house, my brain set on thinking things through, on setting a course of action where no one would get hurt. I held no confidence such a plan existed.

12
CHARLOTTE

Curling in on myself on Nathan's couch, I waited for him to come back from checking on Trina. Being with Nathan hurt Liam. I could hear it in his voice, could *feel* it in the way he'd hung up on me. Guilt rose to choke me, my mind racing.

Liam hadn't stood me up, and I should have thought to call the hospital to check in on him rather than jump to that conclusion. As a surgeon, he would be indisposed sometimes. I only wish I'd considered that before taking off to Nathan's.

I felt certain Liam didn't know Nathan had left because of me, that I'd been a horrible friend and slept with his crush, but the pain in his voice... *Did* he know? Did he assume I was going behind his back again, attempting to seduce Nathan when I knew

Liam wanted our friend more than anything else on the earth?

Not that Nathan had ever belonged to Liam. They'd never been anything more than friends. Nathan didn't "do dick," or so I'd heard from Liam. Still. That didn't give me the right to sleep with my best friend's crush.

Blowing out a heavy exhale, I eyed the hallway while perched on the couch's edge, my heartbeat speeding up a bit as heavy footfalls returned my way.

A red flannel stretched over Nathan's broad shoulders, but he'd buttoned it up while back with Trina, hiding the dark hair across his chest and the trail disappearing into his jeans. Mouth watering, I forced my attention away from his gaze, my heart and mind torn.

"Are you married?" he asked with a grunt while sitting down.

My focus jerked back toward him as he picked up his beer again. "No."

He sipped, not breaking our stare. "No man in your life?"

I hesitated briefly, considering Liam and the path we'd been on prior to learning Nathan had returned. "No," I forced out past the ache in my chest. "There's no man in my life."

Nathan continued to study me, distrust flashing in his eyes before he blinked it away. "So, no kids."

Shoulders wilting, I shook my head, the probability of that never coming to fruition hitting me like a gust of fall wind and sucking away what life I had left in my chest.

"How come no man has stolen you away, locked you in his bedroom, and made you his?"

My core clenched at his blunt words, even though the truth of my answer twisted my stomach. "I'm too fat."

"The fuck you are." His scowl furrowed his dark brows. "You're fucking gorgeous, Char. All those lush curves are perfect for a man like—" He clamped his lips shut for a moment while I held my breath, waiting for him to finish. "For a big and rough man like me," he seemed to force out, his voice strangled. "I was able to stab my dick into your pussy without fear of breaking you."

I blinked, the visuals dampening my panties. He'd never been one to hold back on the filthy talk, and the memory of his words about how good I'd felt around his *dick*, how wet I'd been, how well we fit together, and how badly he wanted to fill me with his cum flooded my mind as it always did when I sought relief.

"You made me harder than any woman before or after you," he continued, his deep voice sweeping shivers over my skin, "and trust me, I fucking looked. Tall, short, stick thin, twice your perfect size —no one has compared to the memory of your body taking every inch of me."

Oh. Well.

For the first time in my life, a sense of self-confidence about my looks, of self-acceptance over my curves rose inside my mind. He'd called me perfect— twice—and Nathan hadn't ever lied.

I fought off the need to clear my throat, blinking away tears while squeezing my thighs together. "Why did you leave?" I asked, needing to hear it from the mouth he'd devoured me with while *stabbing* me with his hard length.

His jaw worked, twitching his beard I wanted so badly to trail my fingertips over. "Because I was confused." Nathan dropped his gaze to the bottle clutched in his big palms. "And I didn't want to hurt Liam."

His words settled heavily in my mind, bringing the clarity I'd missed before. "You knew he loved you," I stated rather than asked.

"Yeah. I did."

We had both betrayed our friend.

The truth should have lessened my guilt, but the gut-churning continued. I couldn't stand the thought of Nathan believing he'd been the one to hurt Liam.

"I talked you into it," I breathed out the words, my throat tight. "I acted like a slut, forcing you to give me what I wanted."

"I gave willingly, Char. It was consensual."

That day still sat as clear as beams of sunlight in my mind. My secret remorse had made it so, warring with my continued desire to relive our short time of intimacy.

"Remember earlier at the lake?" I asked, searching his downturned face, needing him to know *why* I'd begged. "We were dunking each other, playing around."

"I was hard as granite, and you shoved your ass against me. When a woman does that to a man, it's difficult to hide what they've done to him since day one." Nathan finally lifted his head, heat furling from his eyes.

I shifted under his hooded stare but more from discomfort over what I'd done that night than the dampness coating my panties.

"For the first time in my life," I whispered, "I real-ized I—Fatty Boombahlatty, Thick Thigh Charlotte

—turned a man on."

I'd felt wanted. Desirable. In that moment, a sense of power had shattered my insecurities, made me love Nathan all the more, and instilled a craving I couldn't escape.

"I'd been heady with a sense of womanly power I didn't know how to handle," I admitted, "and I knew you wouldn't be averse to taking my virginity if I asked you to."

Nathan's smirk pulsed my core. "Asked?"

I pursed my lips, deep-seated guilt continuing to ride me as hard as the desire for his touch.

"Don't ever feel bad for grabbing my junk and climbing all over my shit while watching a movie that night, Char. I could have made you stop, but I didn't. I chose to fuck you on your parents' couch."

I pushed against the vivid memories, needing to keep my focus on making things right.

"Liam doesn't know. I never told him."

Nathan's beard twitched again, and he nodded. "Probably for the best."

"He's back too, you know."

"So you said."

"He's a surgeon over at the hospital, and he bought that old Victorian over on Elm Street."

Another nod, but I couldn't read his thoughts, his

emotions as I pushed against my own—for both their benefit.

"He would love to see you."

Nathan kept quiet, sipping his beer and avoiding eye contact.

"Do you hate me?" I choked out past the thickness growing in my throat yet again.

His dark gaze stole my breath. "Christ, Char—I could never hate you."

My body yearned to climb onto his lap, and my heart longed to beat in time with his. Yet my mind wanted me to shove Liam in front of him and beg him to love our sweet, selfless friend since I couldn't ever provide all he longed for.

Nathan's return changed things. I wouldn't allow Liam to give me the simple gift he'd offered when I knew his heart wanted someone else. It wouldn't be fair, wouldn't be right.

My hopes for a baby were crushed by a man I still loved, the one man I refused to touch again because I also loved another in equal measure.

"I-I have to go." I hopped up, setting my beer bottle on his coffee table, my emotions so scattered, unsettled I didn't know what to think or feel. Arousal. Disappointment. Guilt. Happiness…

"Char."

"I hope you and Trina like the cookies." I hurried out the front door, taking care to not slam it and wake up the little girl again. Nathan didn't follow after me or call to stop me.

And I told myself I didn't want him to. Liam deserved his love—not me.

13
NATHAN

I pulled on my beard, ears straining for the sound of tires on the driveway and the fading engine of Char's compact car.

No way she knew I'd been fucking Liam. He'd never told her, same as she hadn't let him in on the fact we'd fucked too.

"Fuck." I slouched on the couch, tipping my head back to suck down the rest of my beer.

I stared at the drywall patch overhead, my mind running through memories. Char had always been easy to read, unable to hide her crush on me as kids, but she'd kept things on a platonic level until that day—same as me.

Because I'd always known Liam wanted me. He'd had one too many wet dreams in the bed across our room, grunting and whispering my name in the middle of the night. Or maybe he'd jerked off thinking of me, not realizing I could hear every rustle he made under his comforter.

His groans had made me hard as granite—same as Char's curves—and I'd lusted after them both, keeping it secret. Even at sixteen, I'd known I would never be able to choose between the two of them, so I exercised restraint.

But a horny teenager could only take so much teasing, so many heated glances, never mind when the two he lusted after threw themselves at him, begging for his dick.

I cursed again.

Whatever they had going on between them, they'd been holding hands for fuck's sake, had just been shot to shit—I didn't doubt. Char telling me Liam would love to see me and the pain in her eyes said it all. Her damn insecurities made her think she wasn't good enough for me. For him. That, and I knew she preferred Liam's happiness over her own.

But last she'd probably heard, I didn't do dick, so why would she try to step out of the picture in the hopes he and I would get together?

What the fuck did I want from her? From Liam?

"Fuck." Muttering a few more curses, I rubbed a

hand down over my beard and checked the time on my cell.

Nine—not too late to finally unload the shit of my life to a non-involved friend and hope for good advice.

Carissa answered without sleepiness in her voice, and I relaxed back on my couch.

"You never call," she said, a smile in her tone. "Everything alright?"

"Yes and no."

"Well, start talking. I'm here."

I shared my life from the previous twenty-some years, starting at age fifteen when I first met Liam with his sky-blue eyes and shy smile. The plump, pink-cheeked angel who seemed attached to his hip.

Falling for them both.

Fucking them both.

Fleeing south out of cowardice and the regret I'd come to live with.

"You still love them."

"Yeah," I admitted, closing my eyes and scooting downward to tip my head back against the couch.

"You're sure they're not together?"

"Liam's as gay as the sun is hot, and Char insisted, so I'm assuming she's telling the truth."

"You told me they used to hold hands all the time as kids," Carissa reminded me.

I opened my eyes, staring at the dark TV screen. "True, but do adults do that sort of shit?"

"You said Liam's needy."

I snorted a laugh. "He's always been a self-proclaimed needy bitch."

"Then maybe Charlotte is really just his friend, someone he's super comfortable with, someone he takes comfort in."

Carissa had a point, but the bigger question lingered in my head. "So what the fuck should I do?"

"Be their friend again. Maybe have a sit-down, spill-your-guts discussion. Tell them the truth and see where fate takes you."

I cursed silently over the sudden tightening in my gut.

Fate had torn me out of Rhode Island, and fate had put a doctor prick in front of Blakely to keep me from getting in her pants.

"How's Blakely?" I asked, ready to think about something else.

"She and Stewart are on cloud nine."

I considered smiling, happy for Blakely, but couldn't entice my lips to twitch. She'd found someone who didn't mind her baggage—

"No-No!"

Trina's cry pulled me up off the couch. "Gotta go."

"Call me later!" Carissa rushed, and I hung up with a quick goodbye, leaving my unfinished beer on the coffee table to hurry back and check on Trina again.

She sat in the middle of her bed, thumb in her mouth, eyes wide and wet.

"You okay, pumpkin?" I whispered, sitting beside her.

Trina launched herself against my chest, her small hands grasping at my shirt and beard. "Bad dweam."

I hugged her tight and grabbed Lambey from where she'd left her greatest treasure behind—for my arms.

"Come on, little girl." Emotion swelled tight in my chest, and I realized in that moment there was no such fucking thing as baggage. "Uncle No-No will keep you safe."

We snuggled under my blankets until her breaths evened out, and I only slid off the bed to take off my boots and replace my strangling jeans with sweats. A quick lock up of the front door and I paused, eyeing the container of cookies on the table.

The first bite earned a groan. Goddamn, my Char could bake hella good cookies, ten times better than my neighbor's peanut butter ones.

I glanced around the shack's small kitchen, and like a goddamn boot to my gut, longing slammed in to have her there in nothing but an apron, bent over the oven and pulling out a roasted chicken, my hands palming her plump ass cheeks…

Fuck yeah.

But Liam.

Jaw clenched, I grabbed another beer and settled on the couch to drink the ache in my chest away since I couldn't just take off like I'd done twenty years earlier. By coming back to the past, I'd made my bed. I would have to deal with it like Carissa had suggested, no matter my reluctance—or the sure disastrous outcome.

14

LIAM

I slept like absolute shit and was up and out of bed before the sun. While my body attempted to rest and my brain refused that need during the long night hours, I'd come to a conclusion.

Nathan and I needed a resolution, and even though my dick ached at the thought of being beneath him again, I couldn't bear to hope. He'd crushed my heart, and I couldn't afford another. Char and I had made plans, and I wouldn't break them for anything. I would attempt to give her the baby she wanted, regardless of the outcome of my confrontation with Nathan.

That was, if he wanted me after all this time and both of them wouldn't be turned off by the gift I'd promised Char.

Hardly simple, either relationship, but both worth their weight in diamonds. If only there was a way to have Char *and* Nathan.

My hands clenching the steering wheel, I crossed town toward the address a quick internet search had given me. The Oakland home sat back in the woods up a long, steep driveway, and I turned in, steeling myself with a steady inhale.

Less than fifty yards.

Twenty.

The front door opened as I put my car in park alongside an old truck, and Nathan stood on the threshold.

He'd always been a big guy, but he'd turned into a goddamn grizzly. A mere inch or two separated the top of the door jamb from the top of his head. An unbuttoned flannel hung off his broad shoulders, his massive chest lined with dark hair that dipped into sweats hanging off his hips.

No shoes.

Sexy as hell, enough that my dick didn't care I'd jerked off before leaving the house.

He tipped up his head, crossed his arms, and studied me with his dark eyes as I sat unmoving. Staring, rubbing my glossed lips together. Nathan had been everything I'd always wanted, always dreamed about.

He still is—and then some.

My gaze lingered on his massive hands, remembering the feel of his fingers stretching me.

Hell.

Swallowing a rush of saliva, I forced myself to climb out of the car, the hairs on my arms raising from the live wire electricity between us.

He slid his gaze down over me, taking his good old time, and I straightened, tipping my own chin up. I'd put on some weight of my own, but the flashing worry that he might not like my new non-twink body beneath my tight unicorn shirt deflated my pride.

Yet the energy between us remained, drying my mouth and stealing my thoughts.

Whatever I'd planned to say, all the ways I'd dreamed of greeting him, dissipated in my brain, and I stared, waiting for him. However much I didn't want him to control the situation I'd placed us in, he held it—*us*—in his hands.

He'd always dictated the outcomes.

"Liam," he finally grunted my name, and the low rumble from his chest hit my sternum with pure lust.

"Nathan." At least I didn't whisper and my voice didn't shake.

"Coffee?" he asked, his hooded eyes peering into mine, without a doubt seeing clear to my soul, same as always. I'd never been able to hide jack shit from him. Even knowing I wanted him, he asked me in.

My thumping heart turned hopeful. "I'd love some."

"Come on in."

He moved back into the house, and I hurried after him like a long-lost pup, tongue salivating to loll in happiness.

"Char told you I was back." Nathan pulled open a cabinet to get a mug, the flannel stretching tighter across his shoulders. He'd packed on muscle since I'd seen him last, an easy hundred pounds more than my one-eighty.

"Yes."

"She tell you why?"

"Your niece. I would offer condolences for your brother, but I know you don't want them."

Nathan poured me a cup of coffee, muttering a curse at his dead brother. When he turned, his gaze snagged mine again.

Two steps crowded me into his personal space, and I accepted the offered cup, sipping without taking my focus off him. Faint lines lay at the corners of his eyes, and that dark, sexy beard...a lumberjack I lusted to have in my dreams and bed. "You look good, Nathan," I whispered up at him, my voice all needy bitch as usual when it came to him.

"I'm looking old as fuck," he grumbled but didn't back away or seek to put space between us.

"*Hot* as fuck," I refuted, unable to help my flirty smirk while sipping again. "You know," I said, trying for a conversational tone when he didn't respond, "it's been twenty years since you ripped my heart out, and I still haven't gotten over you."

Nathan's beard twitched as though he clenched his jaw, and I couldn't help myself. I reached up and slid my palm along the silken hairs, goosebumps once more rising on my arms.

"Even with other men, I couldn't keep from thinking of you," I murmured. "How you showed me the way it could be. How you took care of me."

"Liam." He half-groaned my name but didn't move.

I set aside my mug and took another step closer, tipping my head back to hold his heated stare that left me feeling more exposed and vulnerable than I'd ever experienced. "Why did you take off like that, Nathan? Were you ashamed of fucking me? Afraid we would be found out and you'd be called a faggot too?"

"I'm not gay."

"You're gay for me."

"Was," he bit out but stayed put.

My hand on his hard chest showed me the heavy, rapid thumps of his heart beneath.

His breath caught, so I glanced down.

"Gorgeous thing, gray sweats," I murmured, my pulse racing as I lifted my focus to his face again. "There's no hiding what you're packing or how badly you want to fuck."

"Liam," he croaked my name.

I smirked up at him, leaning in to rub my body against his. Holy fucking hell, he was hard all over. Big. So damn massive my asshole clenched and mouth drooled. "Yes?"

"You're a fucking tease," he rasped. "Haven't changed in that way one goddamn bit."

I slid my hand from his chest downward, and my sassy smile grew, confidence giving me balls like I'd had back when we were kids and I decided on offering him my virginity. "And you love it." I grasped his dick, leaning into him like the needy whore I was.

He pulsed in my hand, a deep groan rumbling his chest—my only warning.

Those hard, huge hands grabbed my ass, and he hauled me in closer, his hips grinding against mine as he took my mouth.

I melted, pre-cum oozing from the only hard part of my body, my whimpers getting lost in the violence of Nathan's mouth I'd always wanted to taste again.

So much for 'was' gay for me, Nathan Oakland.

15

NATHAN

Fuck him, and fuck those goddamn baby blues I couldn't ever say no to. The grasp of his firm hand caused stars to burst behind my eyelids—I fucking lost my mind, same as the first time he'd touched me. Enticed me. Created an addiction I never thought I'd crave.

I bit on his pouty, strawberry-sweetened lips, shoving my tongue between them to lap at his mouth, suck his breath deep into my lungs. Hunger I hadn't felt in too damn long swelled me to the point of pain, and I groaned at the grip of his hand around my throbbing dick. Dug my fingers into his ass and squeezed, the need to fuck into him balls deep catching me up in a storm of lust I couldn't escape.

I hated that I wanted him. Hated that I wanted

Char, too. Why the fuck couldn't time and space take away the connection I'd always felt for both?

"Missed you," Liam gasped beneath my bruising lips, his words barely registering through the rush in my ears. "Missed us."

Same. Fucking same.

"Unca No-No?"

Liam reacted at Trina's voice in the hallway before I did, jerking away from me and smiling around my hulking form.

Couldn't. Fucking. Move.

My entire body trembled, hands fisted at my sides, my brain telling me to calm the fuck down. I cursed myself for the brief second of considering Trina baggage because I couldn't bend him over the table and take what I wanted.

"You must be Trina," Liam said, his voice steady, flashing pearly whites. He bumped his shoulder against my arm while swerving around me to get to her.

Eyes clenched shut, I twisted toward the counter, grasping the edge with a death grip. I bent a bit, trying to hide my throbbing cock tenting the hell out of my sweats. I needed to get ahold of myself—acting like a goddamn animal.

Christ, the things he does to me.

I glanced over to find Liam squatting in front of Trina.

"Well aren't you just the cutest thing ever."

"No," she sassed back. "Lambey's cuter."

"Oh?"

Trina handed her lamb over, and Liam nodded, accepting her offering.

"You're right," he whispered, petting the stuffed animal's head. "Lambey *is* cuter."

I slouched against the counter, one hand rubbing my chest at the sudden ache and the other covering my groin. Their dynamic brought hope to life in my mind, made me crave him even more.

"She can't talk," Trina told Liam.

"But I'll bet she knows what you're thinking and how you're feeling, doesn't she?" Liam handed Lambey back to her.

"Yeah. Lambey doesn't like Unca No-No's whiskews. They tickley."

Liam chuckled and tugged on her hair.

In went the thumb, and Trina clutched her treasure and blankie tighter. Her little head nodded, eyes big from sleep, same as every morning when she first woke.

"I still think you're pretty cute too," Liam whispered.

Trina smiled around her thumb, the innocence, the acceptance on her little face intensifying that ache in my chest.

"You and I ought to have a nail polish date," Liam told her.

"You paint your fingewnails?"

Liam lifted his hand, flashing pink and purple alternating colors across the tips.

"Spawkles too!" Trina's eyes lit up, her gaze plastered to his hands.

"I'll bring my polishes over some day and give you the full spa treatment, okay?"

"Unca No-No too?"

Liam turned his head, his smile fading as our eyes clashed. "If he wants me."

The heat remained between us, but anger simmered inside me, and there was no fucking way I could hide it.

I was gay for him, no fucking doubt—and after having him in my hands again, I knew I would never be fulfilled by pussy alone. Liam owned a part of me, pieces I'd attempted to bury, and all it had taken was one flirty smile, one sure grasp on my dick, and the taste of his sweet mouth to bring everything back.

But he'd held hands with Char, and even though both she and Carissa assured me it meant nothing, the back of my mind disagreed. They had something between them, something I wasn't about to fuck up—because I loved them both.

"Nathan?" His troubled gaze flickered over my face as he stood. Whatever he saw didn't sit well in his gut. He straightened. "I won't apologize."

"Not asking you to," I bit out.

"So you left because you were afraid—"

"I'm not doing this right now, Liam."

He glanced down at Trina who moved in against my thigh to peer up at him, grinning around her thumb.

"You're right," Liam mumbled, his smile for my pumpkin wobbling. "Can we see each other soon?" Those baby blues once more flicked toward my face.

Yes. No.

Liam swallowed at my lack of a verbal answer and nodded. "You know where to find me?"

Still I stared, not willing to give him anything—promises or otherwise.

Pain flickered across his face, and I turned away, jaw clenched. Confusion, doubt, lust, longing slammed into me—a fucking mess in my goddamn head.

"Okay, Nathan." His whisper ached my chest again. "I get it."

He spun and left, and as the door closed behind him, a sagging exhale released from my lungs.

"Dat your fwiend?" Trina asked around her thumb.

Throat tight, I nodded. "Yeah, pumpkin." My damn voice wavered, and I pushed away the other words wanting to tumble from my lips.

Lover.

An insatiable itch.

Mine.

"How about some toast?" I muttered, dragging my eyes off the closed door.

"Fwench toast!" she hollered, scampering up onto her booster chair. "With maple sywup!"

"You got it, kid."

If only my desires were solved as easily as my little pumpkin's.

16

CHARLOTTE

Liam didn't call me Saturday and didn't answer when I buzzed him later that night.

An emotional wreck and taken to the point of wanting to curse, I texted him Sunday morning.

He still stayed silent.

Antsy feet got the best of me, my curiosity worse than any cat's, and right after my lunch, I hopped in my car to get some answers.

I drove past Liam's house like a stalker but couldn't tell if his car sat in the garage or not. Nothing moved in the windows as I crept by, so I headed across town.

I expected Agatha to be sitting on her front porch. She was—and waved.

"Lovely," I muttered, flashing a fake smile and

waving back. "Mom's going to get a call wondering what I'm doing on this side of the tracks." I let out a heavy exhale. "Just lovely. Cue the gossip and my cell ringing off the hook later today."

Rather than slow to pass Nathan's driveway because the busybody best friend of my mom's would know exactly what I'd come her way for, I continued at my leisurely pace up the road as though I had zero intentions of stopping. I strained my neck while passing Nathan's mailbox and driveway.

No BMW, so no Liam.

I pulled off the road and sat there for a few seconds, considering while chewing on a hangnail. What excuse did I have for swinging by twice within two days? Pick up my cookie container? Offer to watch Trina for him if he had errands to run?

Agatha had already done that, according to Mom. Nathan wouldn't need a second babysitter with her bored backend having nothing to do but be a nosey neighbor on her porch.

"To hell with it," I muttered a half-curse I wouldn't usually let slip past my lips. "I've got to know what's going on."

Once more, Nathan split wood at the side of his house but without a shirt to hide his bulging muscles.

I swallowed harshly, instantly damp between the thighs at the sight of sweat slicking over his torso.

Get a hold of yourself, woman.

I climbed out of the car as he rested the axe on his shoulder, dark gaze reaching across the distance separating us.

"Hi," I called, my steps hesitant. Had I made a mistake in visiting to sate my curiosity? Would being around him only muddle up my intentions to get my two friends together?

Nathan's gaze swept down over my sundress and the flip-flops I'd gone for with the heat of the day. "Hi," he returned my greeting, not moving from his spot.

Fine. Up to me to do the initiating yet again.

"It looks like you turned into a true lumberjack," I said, hoping my smile would entice one of those smirks that fluttered my belly.

His beard didn't so much as twitch until he opened his mouth to reply. "Guess so."

"You took over your brother's tree company?"

"Yes."

I nodded, making note of the pile of unsplit logs that had been cut to length while trying not to wring my hands. "It appears you'll have plenty of firewood for the next couple of years."

"More than enough—found out last week my brother sells it by the cord, so I'll be doing the same."

"You should rent a splitter," I said, flicking my focus back over his sweating upper body.

"There's one out back."

"Then why kill yourself?" I asked with a light laugh that sounded way too breathy, betraying my unease.

"It's a great way to get out my aggression. Stress."

I studied his furrowed brow, realizing small talk wouldn't get me any answers. "How are you doing, Nathan?"

"I was fine," he bit out.

"Was."

He eyed me, still stubbornly withholding information.

"Until I showed up? Or did Liam stop by and put you in a funk?"

"He came over yesterday morning."

Finally *something,* and by the deepening furrow and his gaze moving off me, I knew he didn't appreciate the visit.

I'd been the one to crack open that eggshell. "It's my fault. I told him you moved back home."

"Quit blaming yourself for everything, Char. I'm damn tired of it."

My eyebrows narrowed over his annoyed grunt, my hands finding my hips at the sudden change in tone. "What the hell is your problem, Nathan Oakland?"

His gaze jerked back to me as quick as a rattler strike. "You swore."

"I'm just trying to do what's right. Be kind. Apologize if I've offended, so answer the *damn* question," I snipped, hating the hot and cold battling inside me.

"My problem?" Nathan took a step closer and dropped the axe to the ground, his hands fisting at his sides. "I saw you holding hands with him last Sunday going into the store, and it ripped my fucking heart wide open. And the worst part? I can't decide who I'm more fucking jealous of—him or you."

My jaw unhinged, my annoyance obliterated.

"I left twenty years ago because I was confused as fuck, Char. And seeing you both has brought it all back, but fifty times worse."

Nathan had always been reluctant to let his feelings out, and I'd never once heard him unload like that. Ever. I snapped my jaw shut.

Movement in my periphery tore my focus off his expectant stare, and my smile returned at the sight of the beautiful munchkin I'd seen around town a time or two.

"You must be Trina," I said as she picked her way over scattered tree bark to reach us.

"You pwetty," she said, showing off gaping baby teeth.

"So are you," I told her, my smile widening even as my teacher's mind calculated her need for speech therapy. "I'm Charlotte."

"Like the pig and the web book? Dat's Unca No-No and my favwit."

Heart melted, I glanced over to find Nathan watching her with so much emotion in his eyes that my ovaries sped toward explode mode.

Searing desire swelled in my heart and my eyes stung with tears. All my dreams of love and babies fulfilling my life slammed into me, stealing my breath. I craved Liam's gift—and yet I wanted the same with Nathan.

Self-sacrificing, something I'd never seen in him before, drew me in more than his appearance, and my body physically ached for him. Knowing he wanted us both, same as I did with him and Liam…I understood his pain. The deep-seated longing.

I wondered if Liam knew Nathan loved him like I did, but I wasn't about to crack *that* eggshell. I'd messed up enough, and it would be best for all involved if I sat back and allow the broken heart to come to me in its own time.

Unlike Nathan, I wasn't confused. There was no choice in the matter. I adored both my best friends enough to take myself out of the picture and watch their love hopefully unfold. Which it definitely would once Nathan let Liam in on his little secret.

"Like the pig and web book," I told Trina, my eyes wet while returning my attention to her. "Does your Uncle Nathan read to you every night?"

"Yeah. After bweakfast too."

"He's a good uncle, isn't he?"

"He makes the *best* Fwench toast with lots of maple sywup!" She clasped my hand and tugged me toward three split logs set up like a table and little chairs. "Want some tea? Uncle No-No's fwend gave us cookies. *Chocolate.*"

The way Trina said the last word, I knew she and I stepped on a path of becoming best friends.

Glancing over my shoulder, I found Nathan still standing in the same spot and studying us, his stance more relaxed but his eyes still troubled.

"I can stick around for a while if you need a break."

From her, from me... Please, Nathan. Settle your heart and mind on Liam and make us all happy.

Unable to voice the thoughts choking me, I sat on my log seat and let Trina serve me. Her constant prattle occupied my mind and ears, weaseling into my heart in ways my first graders never had. Unsure if it was because of who looked after her or not, I just went with the flow, accepting my insta-love for the little girl.

If she belonged to Nathan, then they were a bundled package for friendship once he figured out he wanted Liam. I *hoped* it would be Liam, even though the thought of being left behind stabbed at my heart like a sharpened pencil.

"Any place around here to get a good burger and beer?" Nathan asked from where he stood watching us.

"The best? Mel's about twenty minutes south of here. It's Liam's and my favorite place to go."

"Nothing here in town?"

"Not that compares to Mel's, no. Kelly, her cook, makes a mean one, and Mel serves locally brewed beer you would like. Trust me."

"Haven't had a burger in weeks. You sure about sticking around after I spilled my guts like that?"

"It's therapeutic to voice our emotions, Nathan—

and I'm sure." I smiled, trying to shut down the love I felt for him from shining in my eyes. "I've got nothing planned for the rest of the day. Take all the time you need to figure this out. I'm not going anywhere, and we can always talk more later."

He moved past us with a nod, and I stared at his broad back.

"Nathan?" I called after him.

Eyebrow arched in question, he glanced over his shoulder.

"What you saw last Sunday…Liam and I are just friends. It's all we've ever been."

Another brisk nod as though he'd run out of words, and he disappeared into the small house.

"Did you know shit is poopy?"

"Wh-what?" I gasped at Trina's random comment.

"Shit. Unca No-No says it's poopy."

I bit back my laugh. Barely. Nathan might be a good uncle to care for his niece, but I would have to school him on appropriate language for a four-year-old—same as my Mom had done with me.

"It does mean poopy," I told Trina, "but some people don't like that word. It's best to just say poopy, okay?"

"Lambey poopies in the grass."

Laughing, I settled in for what I expected would be a good, long chat about her stuffed animals and their bowel habits.

Turns out, I was right, and twenty minutes later, Nathand took off, his hair still damp from a shower, jeans hugging his ass, and a tight black t-shirt stretched over his upper body.

I drooled, and he drove away, leaving me with the person who'd brought him back into my life.

I'm not sure if I should kiss you or attempt to not fall in love with you too, little girl. Smiling at Trina, I accepted my third cookie from her.

"Will you be my new best fwiend?"

I shifted on my hard perch, knowing neither of us would be going anywhere, anytime soon. "I would love that, sweet girl."

Her toothy grin officially melted what was left of my heart.

17

NATHAN

Mel's was a quaint bar in the middle of nowhere. An old-fashioned bell jingled as I opened the door. Wide, plank floors—fucking ancient—and a low timber ceiling brought on a cozy, sit your ass down and drink vibe.

I slid onto the closest stool, nodding my head at the old man beside me. His watery eyes lingered on me while I checked the place out.

A sweet ass bent over at the bar's far end snagged my attention as the woman grabbed something from a low shelf, but she had nothing on Char.

The cold stare of the badass mother fucker sitting on the other side of the bar beyond her said it all.

Mine, stay the fuck away.

Add in the "67" tattooed on his neck and the ring

on his left hand, and I knew better than to fuck with the guy. I nodded my agreement, and the bartender turned, catching sight of me.

"What can I get ya?" she asked with a big smile, her whiskey-brown eyes alight with happiness as she approached my end of the bar. Sure enough, she had a matching single band on her ring finger as the guy down at the bar's end.

"I heard you've got some good local beer and the best burgers around." I replied, keeping my tone cool and level so her protector didn't think I was hitting on her.

"Both are true."

"Bring it on."

"You got it. Melody Landon, owner and operator." She stuck out her hand. "But you can call me Mel."

The guy at the end with his dark hair streaked with gray still stared me down, so I didn't take her offered hand. "Nathan—and no offense, but I get the feeling your man doesn't like anyone touching his property."

Her cheeks flushing, Mel laughed, dropping her hand. "That's Nicky—*Mr.* Landon—and he'd take it out on me, not you," she said, leaning toward me with a wink, "and trust me when I say I wouldn't mind. At all."

Well, fuck. A bark of laughter escaped me, pulling the watery gaze of the old man again.

"Junior," Mel said to him, "you take it easy on Nathan. Let me feed the man before you start telling your stories."

He mumbled something about the peppery hops keeping his sinuses clear as she poured my beer, and I dipped my head in thanks when she set a frothing pint in front of me.

"Kelly'll get your burger on the grill in no time. Sit tight."

I sipped my beer and glanced around the rest of the bar, taking note of the suits and flannels, and the college-aged kids home for the summer. Mel's place was bustling, two other girls working the floor while Nicky at the end kept watch with his steely blue eyes.

A Fallen Glider MC brother, the tattoo on his neck warned anyone who knew better. I'd been up in Boston enough to avoid him like a damn shark fin in the water.

Mel had herself one hell of a protector. Kinda old for the girl, but as someone in love with two people, I wouldn't be judging who ought to love who.

"Hey, Billy," Mel called as the door jingled, and

my gut twisted as fucking Billy Jenkins found a seat halfway down the bar.

I stared at him as he ordered whiskey, same as Nicky had. Full bottle, one shot glass. Didn't appear Nicky liked the fucker much either, especially when Billy smiled at Mel with a look that said he wanted a whole lot more than the whiskey she set on the bar for him.

Turning my focus back on my beer, I decided to let Nicky handle him. I'd come to Mel's to get away from everyone and everything, not have another goddamn run-in with people from my past.

Not that the fucker scared me. Never had, and my one shot to his gut for bullying Liam back when we were in high school had laid him out flat, crying like a goddamn pussy.

The day Liam had looked at me with more than lust in his eyes. The day I realized I would do anything for my best friend, even swing the gay way because the looks he'd given me made my dick hard and my chest ache.

Country music filtered overhead, and I settled onto my stool, sipping my beer. The old man rambled away about young punk kids, his neighbor's barking dog, and indigestion.

Eventually, I had enough of his bellyaching and

allowed my memory to run through my time spent with Liam and Char. The good, the bad, and the ugly, not that we'd ever had many bad times.

We'd swum in the lake whenever the sun overheated us. Went fishing and camped out beneath the stars a few times. Almost every other weekend, we ended up at the movies. Hell, us two guys even snuggled around her on her couch late into the night whenever her parents had gone out of town. But we'd never crossed lines, never took things outside of platonic even though I'd itched to every damn time we got together.

My burger arrived, and like Char promised, it fucking rocked my world, taking my mind off all things from the past. I focused on greasy beef and the three thick slices of bacon on top.

I finished and ordered another beer, ready to converse with the old badger beside me rather than just listen to his stories.

The bell jingled, and like I stuck a flathead screwdriver in a socket, energy raced through every cell of my body.

I didn't need to turn my head to know Liam had walked in.

Adding in Billy's coughed "faggot" confirmed it.

Rage rose, same as it had all those years ago,

the need to smash dictating action. Without a word, I stood, catching Billy's attention for the first time since he'd ambled in. His eyes widened like goddamn saucers, but he didn't get a chance to shy away. I grabbed the fucker by the back of the head and smashed him down onto the bar, face first.

Blood sprayed, and he let out a groan, slumping to the side as I released his hair. Liam's quiet curse rang through the bar's sudden stillness.

"The fuck's it matter to you who the man wants in his bed?" I asked Billy, hands fisting. "At least he doesn't beat the shit out of his lovers like you do your wife." I spat his way, only having repeated a smidgeon of what Agatha had told me about Billy Jenkins.

The bar stayed silent except for the country singer crooning from a speaker somewhere. Mel stared, her mouth hanging open, towel clutched in her hand.

"Nathan…" Liam whispered from behind me, but with the blood rage still thrumming through me, I couldn't face him.

I pulled a fifty from my pocket, tossed it on the bar, and met Nicky's gaze. "Sorry about the mess."

He nodded, his beard twitching like he fought off

a grin, and raised his shot glass my way. "Feel free to take the trash out when you go."

That, I could do. Gladly.

I grabbed the back of Billy's shirt and half-dragged him toward the exit, my attention finally landing on my best friend.

Liam stood inside the door, his throat working, his eyes wide behind his glasses, and his cheeks a hot as fuck shade of pink.

I clenched my jaw, tearing my focus off him, and he stepped off to the side to let me wrench open the door. A heft of my arms sent Billy tumbling down the two steps leading up to Mel's.

"Want to stick around?" I asked Liam, my heart pumping hard, my dick swelling with the need to fuck something hard and fast.

He shook his head, glancing between me and the groaning man curled on the ground holding his nose. "N-not really."

"Then let's get the hell outta here," I told him, stalking away, my hands fisted at my sides to keep from grabbing him and devouring him right there in the goddamn parking lot.

He followed like the lost puppy he'd always been. The door slammed shut behind him as he scuttled down the stairs, sidestepping around Billy.

"That was fucking awesome," he breathed with shaky laughter as I strode toward my truck.

"Get in."

"But my car—"

"Get the fuck in. We can come back for your car later."

"And if Billy decides to slash my tires?"

"Fuck." I spotted Liam's BMW on the other side of the lot. "Get your damn car."

"Where are we going?" Liam still trotted behind me, but I moved at a brisk pace to keep from an adrenaline fuck in public or lingering rage-induced murder of the asshole I'd left moaning behind us.

"Wherever you want."

"My place?" His tone hinted at more than a couple beers.

Fuck my usual reluctance. I'd had enough and needed to let off some goddamn steam, unleash the tight reins I kept on my lust.

"Yes," I didn't hesitate to answer. I climbed into my truck, shoved the key in, roared the engine to life, and finally looked at Liam who stood rooted beside the driver side window.

Pupils blown wide and face still flushed, he stared, glossed lips parted as though he panted for the same thing I did. My dick in his mouth—his ass. Whichever hole he preferred.

My groin ached, but I simply raised an eyebrow.

He shivered as though coming out of a trance and hurried to his BMW, eyeing Billy who'd pulled himself up onto his hands and knees. A grin stretched Liam's face as he hopped in his car and turned his focus my way.

Quiet descended like a fog, thick and heavy, but did nothing to cool my heated blood. My dick ached with the need to fuck, release tension, and take what I knew Liam would gladly give.

But Char.

I pulled out of the parking lot on Liam's ass, thinking about *having* his ass, and put a quick call through to Char, my mind set on taking what I could.

"Hey," she said, her voice happy, Trina giggling in the background.

"Can you stay a bit longer?"

"Sure. Everything okay?" She fished over my abrupt tone and lack of greeting, but I was done lying.

"I'm going to Liam's."

Char hesitated long enough I knew that truth hurt, but she didn't give me time to ask forgiveness or second guess my adrenaline-induced decision to take what I wanted. "I'm glad."

"Are you?"

"Yes, Nathan. I am. Stay as long as you want, as long as you need. I'll be here when you're ready to come home."

Muttering a thanks and part of me feeling like an asshole, I hung up and clutched the steering wheel tighter.

No way I would be able to go slow or take it easy. I hoped like hell Liam was ready for me, because I planned on fucking him so hard he gave me the tears I wanted to lick off his cheeks.

LIAM

I didn't think I could love Nathan more than I already did.

I wasn't even sure what had happened in the bar when I walked in. Billy must have muttered something about me to set Nathan off like that. While I hadn't been able to look away from Billy fast enough, Nathan's quick rise from his stool captured my stare and held it as he smashed Billy's face onto the bar.

What were the chances he would be there and that I would show up?

Either fate fucked with me or she offered apologies for all of the heartache in my past.

Surely, it was the latter.

Shaky giddiness swept over me as I drove back

toward the empty house I'd left to grab one of my favorite burgers. My insides fluttered like a kid departing for Disney, and my mouth watered like I stared down chocolates and fudge behind a glass case.

The heat in Nathan's quick glance before storming out the door, the sure steps of his feet across the parking lot....

My ass clenched at the thought of his intentions, and I let out another breathy laugh.

His truck filled my rearview mirror, but darkness started to fall, hiding his face in murkiness. Headlights shot on, blinding me, and I turned down my rearview, focusing on the road ahead. The miles wouldn't pass fast enough.

Funny thing, time. When you wanted her to pass, she slowed, and when you wanted her to drag her ass in the sand, she refused.

Twenty minutes felt like twenty hours, but I finally pulled into my driveway, a quick touch to the button on my visor lifting my garage door. I parked and shut the engine down, taking a few extra seconds to breathe slowly, trying to calm my racing heart.

Nathan parked behind me and shot out of his truck before I even got my door open. Half out of the car, I gasped as his hands found my arms and jerked me upright.

He took my mouth in a bruising kiss, and same as the morning before, I melted against him, whimpering at the hardness, the bulk of him overshadowing my smaller size.

I'd never felt so sheltered, so protected.

So loved.

"Inside," he said and cursed, letting go of me so quickly I stumbled back, almost falling into my car's open door.

"When you get all alpha growly and shit…fuck, Nathan." I let out a shaky giggle. "You make my ass ache to be filled."

"Inside. Now."

My heart thumped so damn hard in my chest, I feared it seizing, but I managed to shut the car door and stumble up the stairs leading into the house.

The heat of Nathan smothered my neck, and before I blinked, he spun me. My back hit the door as he took my mouth again.

Devouring. Biting and licking.

Weakening my damn knees.

"Nathan," I moaned as he scraped his teeth along my jaw, his whiskers tickling in a way I never expected to love. *Crave* took on new meaning.

"I know what you need," he whispered roughly against my ear, ripping at his jeans.

Hands shaking, I kept my head tipped against the door and fumbled to release my own dick.

Heated breaths, frantic mouths eating at one another, we both wrapped our hands around our throbbing dicks shoved together. His deep grunts and groans while rubbing against my length caused pre-cum to dribble at the tip, coating our hands.

My legs shook. Stomach fluttered with the wings of a thousand butterflies.

With a curse, Nathan grasped my ass and yanked me up into his arms, holding me like I weighed no more than a kid.

My dick slid away from his as I wrapped my legs around his waist. His grunted, "Bedroom?" made the loss of pressure on my aching length fine as fuck in my head.

"Upstairs," I rasped. "Door at the end of the hall."

He stomped up the stairs without an ounce of effort, and I clung to the massive bulges of his arms, sliding my hands up over his beard, into his hair. I panted against his mouth, anxious to stretch around his thrusting length and feel the heat of him erupt deep inside my ass.

"I want you bare," I told him and swallowed at the

heat in his dark eyes as he kicked my bedroom door in.

"Gonna fuck you raw, Liam."

"Yes."

A quick, gnashing of teeth and bruising lips and we stepped back as one, ripping the clothes from our body.

I hopped on the bed first and grabbed the bottle of lube from my bed stand while he kicked off his jeans. Dropping to my knees, I lifted my ass, just like he'd claimed to love twenty years ago.

Nathan's weight dipped the bed behind me, and his meaty paw grasped my thigh. He tossed me over onto my back without any effort. "I want to see your face when I take you."

My heart swelled inside my chest, and my eyes stung with tears. I'd dreamed—fantasized—of watching him while he fucked me. Fumbling with the bottle, I let out a few curses. Couldn't get the damn cap open fast enough. "Fuck!"

"Needy little twink." Nathan took the lube from me and flipped the top without effort, his hands steady as a surgeon's.

"I'm not so little anymore," I whispered up at him, lust for his touch trembling me from hair to toenails.

Nathan dribbled lube onto his palm while sliding

his dark gaze over me from mouth to spread legs and back up again. "No, you're not."

I shot him a saucy smirk, even though my pulse pounded in my neck. "Do you still think I'm sexy?"

He grasped his jutting dick and coated himself in lube with one downward swipe, tossing the bottle aside. "What do you think?" His low voice tightened my balls, and I licked my lips, watching the head of his dick disappear beneath his palm and reemerge again with another downward stroke.

"I think I want that monster so far up my ass I can't breathe."

"Fuck, Liam." Nathan squeezed the base of his dick before releasing it and shoving two slick fingers straight into my hole without warning.

Relaxing, I let him in, my teeth finding my lower lip as our gazes held. His hooded eyes spoke of passion I'd experienced only with him—on my knees, my face against the ground. I wanted to drown in the dark of his eyes, get lost in the black pupils leading directly to his soul.

"Kiss me when you fuck me this time," I told him, lifting my hips as he shoved a third finger into my hole, the stretching sting an absolute delicious sensation. He rubbed along my prostate, and I cursed, grabbing hold of the base of my dick to keep from shooting all over my chest.

"Nathan," I moaned and licked my lower lip, my ass squeezing around him. "Please…I'm ready."

He removed his fingers and rubbed the thick head of his dick against my hole.

I wanted to pause time in that moment. Hold his gaze. Soak in the passion in his eyes, memorize the pressure building against my ass as he flexed his hips.

Both our breaths caught as he pushed, breaching my tight ring.

Connected, for the first time in twenty years, and with how he looked at me, I knew he felt the same, bonded far beyond the physical.

"Let me in, Liam." His voice rumbled, pebbling my skin, and he started to sink in farther. "Every goddamn inch."

"Yes." I whimpered at the lush burn in my ass as he planked, stretching me. "Always." I wrapped my arms around his back, my heels finding his ass and pulling him in. Deeper. So damn deep, I *couldn't* breathe.

Filled to the brim with Nathan—body and heart. Tears once more stung.

"Fuck," he groaned through clenched teeth, and I

lifted my head, taking his mouth like I'd always dreamed of doing while he was buried inside me.

Fuck, indeed.

He dragged out and slammed into my ass so hard I saw stars. Lost my breath again. Hips snapping, balls slapping, he fucked me into my mattress like no man had done before, overwhelming my thoughts and my instincts to protect my heart and body.

My ass burned over his assault, and I writhed. Whimpering beneath him, I felt sure I would come without touching my own dick straining between our hardened abs.

"Gonna fill you with my cum, Liam."

"God, yes," I gasped, turning my focus between us as he pushed onto his hands, watching his glistening length appear and disappear with every hard stab into my ass.

"You love my cock in your ass."

"Fuck, yes."

"Tell me how much, Liam." He held my gaze and thrusted, heavy pants between grunts, his hops-laced breath fanning my face.

Did he get caught up in the dirty talk, or did he really want to know how much I craved him?

I grasped his whiskered cheeks and pulled him down once more. The need to show him the truth became more important than tossing out words I didn't want him to think I spewed in a lust-crazed moment.

Lifting up to meet his thrusts, I made love to his mouth, licking and biting, moaning at the snap of his hips. The heat, the sweat of his abs crushed my dick against my own body, and every drive forward rubbed me just right—so fucking right.

My balls seized, and my throat tightened. "Gonna come," I gasped out against his mouth.

A deep groan rumbled his chest as he lifted once more to watch me. "Give it to me."

Dark, hooded eyes. Passion and lust enough to fuel the type of adrenaline rush that wrecked a man's soul

Yes I'll give it to you—anytime, anywhere.

Spunk shot out of me like a geyser, smearing between our skin as he lowered over my body, thrusting harder, sliding my back along the mattress.

Teeth clenched and head tipped back, I rode the waves rushing through me, emptying my balls between our clasped bodies. Still, he slammed into me with brute force.

"Liam. Fucking Christ... *Fuck.*"

The tears returned as my climax lessened enough to focus on his face, mere inches from mine.

Emotional energy radiated between us, and I drank in his panted curses, my heart and body in overload. "Nathan…"

A hot tear slid from the corner of my eye, and he leaned down, capturing it with his tongue—and he fucking detonated inside my ass, every burst of wet heat like a brand on my insides.

He didn't claim me in words, but Nathan's crushing arms, his tongue along my cheek, his grunts against my ear…

Fate had handed me heaven, and no way in hell was I letting go.

CHARLOTTE

He's with Liam.

I snuggled on the couch with Trina, reading Charlotte's Web and fighting to keep my tears locked inside. Joy should have lit my insides, should have wiped away the guilt I'd had hanging on my shoulders since I seduced Nathan all those years ago.

Instead, I constantly swallowed against the tightness creeping up my throat. I widened my eyes to keep the stinging to morph into droplets of salt water that would drip onto my new friend's hair I'd brushed until it shone.

Liam and I had embarked down a path together, and being with Trina reminded me every second of what I wanted, what he'd offered. Our unfulfilled, newfound desire for one another. Would he still follow through with the gift of his sperm if he and Nathan ended up together? Were my chances for a child ruined because I loved two men enough to want their happiness more than my own?

If I were truly such a selfless friend, I would focus on their future, not lament what I might lose.

Trina had told me twice she loved me as much as Lambey.

My heart had been in break mode for hours, and I longed to wrap her up in my arms and smother her with kisses. I wanted to keep her forever. I wanted to keep her guardian forever too. And Liam.

Forcing a smile, I rested against Nathan's comfortable couch and read another chapter. I realized Trina's thumb had popped from her mouth and her grip on her stuffed animal had gone lax.

I'd already done the bath time thing with her, so I set aside the book, picked her up, and carried her into her bed. Nightlight flicked on, I stood over Trina and watched her sleep. So innocent.

And now, so very much loved.

Tears welled in my eyes, hazing over the sight of the little girl. Nathan had always been protective, but to see his adoration for his pumpkin atop such an already alluring characteristic, I knew I had it bad.

Doomed. To a life of loving children from afar in my classroom. Without Liam, my students would have to suffice. Perhaps it was time to look into other options. Fostering. Adopting, if I could save up the money.

Someday, I promised myself, one way or another I would have a child I could love how I wanted to. Unconditional and forever.

My cell twinkled from my bag back in the living room, so I left the little girl to rest, keeping her door cracked open like Nathan had done the first time I'd visited.

Sighing at the name on the screen, I swiped to answer and sank onto the couch. "Hi, Mom."

"Are we in a better mood today?"

"Yeah." I stared out at the darkening sky, snuggling against the pillow that smelled like Nathan. "Sorry about the other night."

"Aggie called."

Of course she did. Even annoyed, I couldn't help but smile a bit. "That so?"

"She said you drove past a few hours ago."

"I did."

"Well." Mom could smell gossip a mile away, and her breathy tone let me know she was ready to launch into fifty-question mode. They came fast and furious, only allowing me one-worded answers.

Yes, I'd gone to visit Nathan.

No, it wasn't the first time I'd seen him.

Yes, I'd heard he'd been at the grocery store but kept to himself.

Yes, I'd seen little Trina, and yes, she smiled and had put on some healthy weight.

Yes, Nathan looked good, but I didn't tell her I'd always thought so.

Add in the extra breadth of his chest, the hair on his chest and arms, the muscle…the beard I'd imagined having between my thighs… I sniffed the pillow I clutched against my belly, my eyes closing.

"Charlotte?"

Clearing my throat, I shifted on the couch. "He's not here. I sent him down to Mel's for some alone time."

"One of my girls said she was driving by Liam's a little while ago. He and Nathan pulled into the driveway, Nathan's truck right behind Liam's. And Nathan followed him into the garage and kissed him like he'd been starving on an island for the last twenty years."

My heart squeezed, and I clenched my eyes shut.

Because he had.

He loved Liam as I did. Hearing of a kiss like that left no doubt in my mind.

I'd done the right thing, so why did I want to curl up in a ball and die?

"It's too bad he likes men," Mom said, not seeming to care I'd gone silent. "I really had high hopes you could get him into bed."

"Mom!" I snipped.

"What? There are no men in this town worthy of my only little girl—"

I'm not so little.

"—and to have both of your best friends, two men I know you've always loved, come back within weeks of one another, and they fall for each other rather than you…"

I swallowed hard.

Mom went silent while I gathered myself together. "Oh, honey. I'm so sorry. Here I am chatting away, not even thinking about how you must feel about all of this."

"I'm good, Mom," I lied, hating that my voice sounded like a shredding machine. "I sent Nathan out hoping he would run into Liam. They deserve one another, and nothing would make me happier than seeing them together."

"People around here might not care for two men publicly loving on each other."

"That's their problem. You know besides Dad that no better men live on this earth. They'll be lovely together." My lips tilted upward even as a tear slid down my cheek.

"If either was aware of how much you loved them both," Mom stated with a sigh, the disappointment in her voice as thick as my own.

Nothing would change. I wouldn't allow it.

My legs shook as I stumbled into Liam's bathroom to get a warm, wet towel to wash us up. Sparkling clean. Marble. Various showerheads in a massive walk-in. Liam had cash coming out his ass.

He also had my cum dripping from his hole when I went back to him, and the sight swelled my dick again.

Eyeing my swinging length, Liam smirked. "I'm going to need a little bit before you shove into my ass again, but you can have my mouth if you want."

The thought of Liam's mouth on my dick stiffened me fully.

Lips in a thin line, I cleaned the cum from his chest first before wiping between his ass cheeks. He allowed me to care for him, the heat of his focus on my averted face itching me in so many damn ways I didn't know what to do.

I went for tossing aside the towel and laying down on my back beside him. Rather than curl against me like he used to do beneath the stars out in the hay field with his palm atop my heart, he slid between my legs, pressing them wide to make room for his body that had filled in perfectly.

Holding my gaze, he grasped my dick and licked over the head, his tongue flicking. Teasing.

Teeth clenched to keep in my groan, I lifted my hips, needing what he offered.

Pink lips parted, he took me into his mouth.

"Fucking Christ!" I bowed off the bed, and he hummed down along my length, clear to the base. His throat worked around my dick—he fucking swallowed. "Fuck, Liam. Fuck."

Grabbing hold of his ears, I took what he offered, yanking him back down harshly when he backed off. My balls tightened up with every gag noise I ripped from his slobbering mouth.

Drool dribbled from his lips, coating and dripping from my balls, and still I fucked his face, our gazes locked.

He loved me. His eyes stated it clearly, no hesitation, no holding back, and my heart ached more than my balls did. He cupped and tugged them down a bit, taking me off the edge, but I couldn't slow. Couldn't let him up for air.

The need to blast down his throat rocked my hips.

His fingers found my ass—and I jolted to a stop, holding him tight against my groin.

I knew he couldn't breathe, but he rimmed my asshole with his fingertip, a place no man, no woman had ever touched.

Swearing, I slowly lifted his head, his tongue and teeth scraping over my length and causing me to grit.

The second I let him pop off my dick, he murmured, "I'm the first one to touch you here?".

"Yes," I rasped out, still clutching his ears, my body shivering with every feather-like pass of his fingertip over my puckered hole.

"You don't know what you're missing out on."

I wasn't so sure. I liked his ass good enough. Didn't need a dick shoved up my own.

Liam pulled his hand away, sucked on his finger, and went back to rimming me, all the while holding my gaze. Teasing me with his narrowed, sassy eyes and a smirk. Testing my reluctance with every swipe over my puckered hole. Eventually probing and whispering, "Let me in, Nathan."

A mere fingertip slid past my ring, and I growled, clenching my hole around him.

"See?" he whispered with another sassy smirk I wanted to lick off his face while he pushed in a bit farther. "But I'll make it even better." He closed his mouth over my leaking dick again and ripped a deep moan from my chest.

Holy fucking Christ...

Wet heat surrounding my dick, a slick finger rubbing inside my ass...

"Gonna come," I grunted.

He hummed around me and twisted his hand, the pad of his finger hitting me deep in a spot that sent lightning crashing through my brain.

"Fuck!"

"Mmm," he agreed around my dick, and I shoved into his throat.

"Swallow," I rasped out through clenched teeth and shot endless ribbons of cum into his willing mouth, every rub of his finger in my ass seeming to entice more spunk up through my dick. My body jerked beneath him, my breaths in grunts, gasps, until he emptied my balls.

"What the fuck was that?" I muttered, falling lax against his bed.

He slid his finger from my ass, and I winced, but his soft kisses up my abs eased the slight sting.

"That," he said, flicking his tongue over my nipple while wiping his finger off on my sheet, "was me milking your prostate."

"Fuck, that felt good."

"Feels even better when it's a thick, juicy cock doing the rubbing." He finally curled against my side where I wanted him, his palm atop my heart.

I grunted a noncommittal reply, slowing my breath along with every heartbeat radiating upward against his hand. Quiet descended, and I closed my eyes, just feeling the emotions tugging me toward him, the fading sting in my backside, the warmth of his skin and hard muscle pressed against me.

Contentment.

"Your cock felt better than I remembered," Liam murmured, breaking the stillness, his lips on my shoulder. "Twice as good since we were face to face and you let me kiss you."

"I've never wanted another man," I admitted. "Never had another man but you."

"Good." His snipped reply made my chest ache as he twirled my hair there with his fingertips.

"I never kissed you while fucking because I thought giving you more than my dick in those moments would turn me gay."

"Is being gay for me so bad?"

"No." I didn't hesitate to reply and wrapped my arm around him, tugging him tighter to my side. "You fit against me like you belong here," I said, my rumbled tone sounding resigned to my own ears.

Liam didn't reply to my statement, and silence settled again, allowing thoughts outside of lust and satisfaction to filter back in. What I'd done all those years ago, why I'd left. The longing for and rightness I'd felt with more than just him.

"I fucked Charlotte the night before I left for Rhode Island," I heard myself say, ready to spill like Carissa had suggested.

Liam's hand on my chest stilled, his hot breath no longer caressing my shoulder.

Staring at the ceiling of his bedroom, I considered what I'd allowed him to do to my body, touching me in ways I swore no one ever would. Then spewing words after emptying my dick down his throat.

Secrets I'd never intended to tell.

Feelings I'd never wished brought into the open.

But Liam made me crave things I never had, never expected to want.

"I left because I loved you both and couldn't stand the thought of having to choose," I admitted, my voice a whisper.

My not-so-twink man stayed stiff against me, but his breath left. "You fucked Charlotte."

"Yes."

LIAM

"She never told me," I stated through the sudden ringing of my ears, my chest aching but for a whole different reason. Charlotte hadn't been honest with me for years. She'd given herself to Nathan, knowing how much I loved him.

"She probably didn't tell you because she loves you." Nathan's words only made my heart hurt more.

If Charlotte loved me that way, she never would have gone behind my back and fucked you.

"She didn't know *we* were fucking," Nathan said, as though he could hear my thoughts. "So it's my fault. I loved you both enough to take what you willingly offered, even though it was a selfish, dick move."

I pushed up onto an elbow, and Nathan shifted his head my way. "You love her still."

He didn't answer, but he didn't need to. His dark eyes gave me the confirmation I expected.

"And me?" I needed to know how badly I'd fucked things up by hopping right back into the sack with his delicious ass.

His beard twitched as though he clenched his jaw. Was he unwilling to answer to keep from breaking my heart? He'd come for me—twice—with an intensity I'd never witnessed before, but had it been only for lust's sake?

He'd admitted being gay for me wasn't so bad. Said I fit against his side like I belonged there, and he had yet to release his hold on me.

My throat tightened as I recognized the truth in his non-answer.

Nathan Oakland still very much loved two people, and it tore him in half.

I'd promised my best friend my sperm to give her what she wanted, but with Nathan back home and available, she would prefer him over a gay man. Bi— or whatever. Laying my hand over Nathan's heart, I considered the breadth of him, the sheer mass of his body.

He loved her. My virile, gorgeous bear of a lover loved *her*.

He could give her the type of big, robust babies I could only ever dream about offering.

And because I loved them equally, I would make his decision easier. I would let them both go.

"I have a surgery at six tomorrow," I lied, letting out a heavy exhale as though exhausted, and stretched out onto my back.

Nathan rolled to face me, but I closed my eyes, forcing a satisfied smile, even though my heart broke.

"Don't bullshit me." His low voice pebbled my skin, but I focused on my sweet Char's face in my mind. The heartache she'd been through trying to fulfill her dreams.

"I'm not lying—I do have to perform a surgery early tomorrow morning." *Just not at six.*

He grasped my chin in his meaty paw and turned my head his way. "Look at me."

Unable to deny him, my eyelids popped upward on their own.

Dark eyes studied my face, and I attempted to breathe steadily beneath his scrutiny, even though my breath wished to cut off and hold until he finished rooting out whatever he hoped to find.

"Fine." Nathan grunted and rolled off the bed, the muscles of his backside snagging my attention as he bent to pick up his clothes. "Want me to lock up on my way out?"

"Please." I barely managed a squeak past the thickness growing in my throat.

He shoved one leg into his jeans then the second before turning to face me. "Why are you doing this, Liam?"

Because you deserve her. She can give you a life in this shit town that wouldn't be under constant judgement.

"Did you have a good time tonight?" I asked instead of stating the truth.

His beard twitched again, but he nodded.

"Thank you for sticking up for me at Mel's."

"Anytime."

"Thanks for the use of your dick too. Brought back some good memories, didn't it?" I went for flirty and sassy but failed due to the stinging in my eyes I blinked away.

"Anytime," he stated again, his dark gaze promising he'd give it to me again. I only had to ask.

I offered a saucy smirk, my lips pressed tight, and he left me to my tears.

~

"NATHAN ASKED me out to dinner tomorrow night." Charlotte's quiet voice over the cell stung my eyes worse than any punch to the nose ever had.

I poured a little more creamer into my morning coffee while swallowing down my heartache. "And?" I asked once I could control my voice.

"I told him no, of course."

Placing a smile on my face I hoped would come across the line, I asked, "And why would you do that? We both know you've been in love with him forever."

"So have you."

The truth I'd learned the night before after Nathan fucked me into the mattress returned to my mind, bringing along anger over not being what either of them needed.

"But I can't give him what he wants, what you can," I told her, slamming my fridge door a little harder than necessary.

"And what's that?"

"A normal lifestyle. A relationship, a marriage that would be accepted up here in the sticks."

"There's a rumor going around that he kissed you in your garage last night."

I leaned against my kitchen counter with one

hand, pinching the bridge of my nose and displacing my glasses with the other. "It meant nothing."

"Your voice begs to differ."

Letting out a heavy exhale, I pushed to stand upright, grabbed my coffee, and made for the stairs. "I have surgery in a few hours."

"Liam."

"He realized that I'm not what he wants, Char. He told me he loves you—he always has." The truth choked me, and I waited, praying she would finally be honest with me.

"Is that all he told you?" she finally asked, her voice a whisper, almost fearful.

"No."

"Damnit." Her whispered curse made it through the line.

Her betrayal had stung, but our history together softened the blow. Besides, I knew more than anyone how irresistible Nathan Oakland was.

"Look, Char." I walked into my bathroom, eyeing myself in the mirror, knowing what I was about to say was utter bullshit, but it was best for everyone involved. "He'll never be my knight in shining armor. He doesn't want me that way."

His eyes and kisses told me otherwise.

My throat closed up, but I forced the words to

continue. "He took off all those years ago because I threw myself at him, and he hated himself for what we did when he loved you all along. He felt like a cheating piece of shit and decided his scholarship was a better choice than facing your broken heart."

Utter fucking bullshit.

"Oh," she breathed, and I turned away from the mirror, eyes clenched shut.

"Call him, Char. Go out with him. Make him a happy man, and maybe he can give you what you've wanted your whole life."

"What about that gift you promised me?" Her voice cracked.

My lips twisted in a half-smile in attempt to keep my own sadness under wraps, but the thought of losing out on being with Char, filling her belly with a baby, sliced deeper than any scalpel. "It never would have been a simple gift, no matter how much I longed to make it one," I whispered once I found my voice. "I like men, Char, always have."

"But you like me too."

"Yes, but I need more." Finally, a truth from my lips. I loved her dearly, but I also loved Nathan. I couldn't have them both, but I would find a sense of contentment in seeing them together.

"That hurts, Liam," she whispered with an agonized breathlessness that fucking *killed* me.

"It's the truth." A tear slid down my cheek. "Please make him happy. If not for his sake and yours, you can do it for mine too."

"I love you, Liam," she choked out. "You know that, right?"

"I love you too."

2 2

CHARLOTTE

I got off the phone with Liam and had a good sob fest, tears, snot, and all. Curled in my robe, still in bed, I'd called him the second I'd woke.

Nathan had come home the night before, his hair a mess as though he'd been tugging on it, his eyes troubled. I didn't tell him the rumor I'd heard from Mom, and he didn't have much to say other than a thank you and to ask me back for dinner the next night.

Although my chest stung to smell Liam's new cologne on Nathan, I told myself to be happy at what I'd accomplished—getting my two best friends together.

But Liam's words hit me like a slap to the face.

Nathan's quietness, his more than usual reserved manner from the night before made sense.

They must have had a falling out, and oh how I wished to have been a fly on that wall. Not knowing what had transpired but being in between the two emotionally was wrecking my heart.

Add in the ruined path Liam and I had been on… the tears wouldn't stop. He and I hadn't ever fought, but we found something in our way, a hurdle not easily overcome. We admitted our love for one another before hanging up, so I didn't believe our friendship was over at least. Perhaps in time, things could go back to normal.

I blew my nose for the fifth time and sprawled back on my bed, my head aching and pounding at the same time.

I'd told Nathan no to dinner, even though I'd yearned to say yes.

Liam wanted me to change my answer, but I was in no place to talk to Nathan just yet. Finding out he loved me, that he had for all these years, hearing he'd taken off out of guilt for messing around with our best friend made me crave a hot fudge sundae with extra cherries on top.

I longed to wrap Nathan up in my arms and tell him

I forgave him. Tell him I loved him. He needed to know I didn't care about his past choices with Liam—heck, I didn't care they'd kissed in his garage the night before.

The thought of them lip-locked kinda turned me on.

I considered my body's reaction. Imagined it in vivid detail in my mind, teeth and tongues, both of their heated groans and grasping hands.

Yep. Definite arousal between my thighs.

"Ugh." I climbed off my bed and ambled toward the shower. "Get your head on straight, Char. Figure out who the heck you want, then make whichever phone call that entails."

Three hours later, I still had no clue what my heart and body wanted, but when my cell rang, Nathan's name popping up on the screen, peace swept in, giving me my answer.

I knew what was best for him, for me, since Liam had taken himself out of the picture. Heart still aching, I decided it was time to see if Nathan would stand me up.

"Hey," I couldn't keep the sting of loss from my voice.

"Trina's in the ER." His voice shook, and my heart slammed in my chest.

The stirring threesome turmoil vanished from my head.

"What happened? Is she okay?" I ran to the foyer, my flip flops slapping the floor, and grabbed my purse.

"She got hit on the head pretty hard. Bled all over the fucking place." His voice broke again, the sound causing my eyes to well up. "I need you, Char."

I tore my front door open. "I'm coming, Nathan. I'll be there in ten minutes, okay?"

"'Kay."

Tears slid down my face as I hopped in my car and backed out of my driveway.

"Get yourself together, woman," I chided myself, swiping at my cheek while racing up the road. "Nathan needs someone in control, not an emotional basket case."

Worry for Trina ate at my stomach, and until I pulled into a parking space at the hospital, I felt sure I would hurl my breakfast. I stormed into the ER, swallowing and walking with purpose, purse clutched at my shoulder. My head swiveled as I searched for Nathan.

He sat on the far side of the waiting room, bent forward, head in his hands. As though he felt my presence, he looked up, his dark eyes piercing through me and seizing my breath.

I loved him. Completely and utterly, without question.

He stood and strode toward me before I could move, and the second he pulled me up against his chest, his mouth against my hair, I closed my eyes.

Home.

I basked in his warmth, his embrace for a moment longer before focusing once more on my fear for Trina.

23
NATHAN

I hugged Char tight against my chest, breathing in her sweetness, finding comfort in her softness. She rubbed my back, making shushing noises, and I realized I cried like a bawling baby in the ER.

Couldn't find two fucks to give though. My little pumpkin…

Char pulled away and grasped my hand, leading me back to the chair I'd been sitting in. "Tell me what happened, Nathan."

I slumped into the chair, closed my eyes, and inhaled until it hurt. A quick swipe across my face rid me of the tears. "I was outside splitting wood, and she was playing tea party close by. I thought she was far enough away, Char." My voice caught at the memory of Trina running in my periphery, but my downward chop couldn't be stopped. The split log had flown out sideways.

Hit her in the forehead.

My eyes clenched shut against the visual replaying in my head, a shudder wracking through me.

She'd gone down like a bag of bricks without making a sound, but I screamed enough for both of us.

Fighting off the continued adrenaline shakes, I managed to spew out what had happened. My lack of focus being what caused it—not that I let on about what my fucking brain had been caught up in.

Troubled thoughts over loving and wanting two different people.

"She was awake when the ambulance got there, but the blood, Char. So damn much..." I swallowed hard, blinking against more tears.

Charlotte squeezed my hand, and I laced my fingers through hers, holding on tight.

The doors leading back into the ER opened, and the doctor who had rushed to Trina when they'd brought her in glanced around.

I hopped to my feet, dragging Char along with me, my heart once more pounding.

"Mr. Oakland," the doctor stated upon catching sight of me.

I nodded, teeth clenched to keep hold of myself.

A small smile lifted his lips, and my breath left in a rush. "She's going to be okay. A small concussion, but no bleeding beyond the laceration on her forehead."

"Thank fuck," I gasped out, tipping my head back toward the ceiling, eyes opened wide to keep from spilling damn tears down my cheeks again. Relief sagged my shoulders, and I pulled Charlotte against me. She wound her arms around my middle, her touch, her presence as much of a comfort as the doctor's words.

"She'll be fine to go home in a little bit, and one of the nurses will go over her discharge papers with you."

I nodded, breathing a heavy exhale, ready for my fucking nerves to settle completely.

"Nathan!"

Liam's voice caused me to whip my head around. He hurried across the waiting room, still in his scrubs, concern etched in his brow. His eyes…fuck, his eyes were filled with the same fear I'd been swamped with since I'd split that damn log. "I heard what happened—is Trina okay?"

"She will be."

He pulled up short of me and Char by about three feet, letting out a quick sigh of relief, but he felt too far away.

I reached out, grabbed hold of his shirt, and yanked him against my other side. He stiffened at my knee-jerk reaction but melted within seconds, his arms, like Charlotte's, winding around my middle.

Between my two lovers, my head chilled the fuck out. Finally.

I'd never felt more comforted, more safe. Ten times better than being alone in my fear and roller-coaster emotions.

In all my selfish thoughts, that was how I'd always wanted us to be.

If only things could remain this way.

24

LIAM

I breathed in the sweat and ozone clinging to Nathan's shirt, my nose catching whiffs of Char's sweetness.

Divine. Absolute heaven.

My dick twitched in agreement, but I pushed away lustful thoughts, considering our situation and surroundings.

A shudder rippled through Nathan like a release of pent-up tension as Doctor Lynch walked back through the doors, leaving the three of us alone in our corner of the waiting room.

"She's going to be okay," Nathan repeated, and I hugged him tighter. The back of my hands brushed across Char's breasts where she snuggled in close too.

A thought flittered through my brain, but it dissolved just as quickly as Char stepped back from Nathan's side. I did the same, seeing as how he didn't belong to me.

"I'd just gotten out of surgery when I heard Trina was in the ER. What happened?" I asked, shoving my hands in the pants pockets of my blue surgical scrubs.

Nathan rubbed a hand over his beard and gave me a quick summary of his mistake. The fact he blamed himself was clear given the tightened creases around his eyes and the downturn of his lips.

"It was an accident," I told him in a firm tone. "And she's going to be fine."

He met my stare, and the same affection and love I'd felt from him the night before hit me hard in the chest and groin. Longing to press against him again, snuggle along his hard body, and offer what comfort I could snagged my breath and didn't let go.

I glanced at Charlotte to find her watching us, her brow furrowed. She didn't believe the lie I'd told her.

Guiltily, I turned to find Nathan had turned his focus on her too.

The same love shone on his face, the type I felt inside every time I looked on our best friend.

Friends. Lovers.

That flitting thought from seconds earlier returned with full force. A goddamn epiphany that brightened my world with the answer we needed. The answer to our heartache. Giddiness damn near floored me, but I managed to stitch my happiness up tight, a mere smile escaping.

"Dinner," I said, my tone not allowing for argument. "My place. Both of you—Trina too."

"Not tonight," Nathan said. "I'm taking my pumpkin home and wrapping her in bubble wrap for the next fourteen years."

Charlotte touched his forearm, her smile and soft handling seeming to calm the protective bear. "We were supposed to have dinner at your place—"

"You said no," Nathan muttered.

"A girl can change her mind," I tossed out, uninvited to the conversation but giving my two cents. Charlotte eyed me in a way that made me wonder if she'd caught onto the answer that had lit my life to the bursting point. "Tell you what. You two take Trina home. I'll swing by after work with the pizza and the makings for hot fudge sundaes."

Charlotte and Nathan studied one another for a few seconds while I held my breath.

"Come on, you two," I pushed. "It'll be like old times. I even have The Blair Witch Project on DVD."

"No. No freaking way," Charlotte said, shaking her head, and Nathan and I chuckled.

"You can bury your face in my chest," Nathan offered.

"And I'll hold your hand," I added, "Just like old times." How had I not considered it before?

My two best friends continued to look at one another.

"So, is that a yes?" I asked, my voice breathless, my smile hopefully infectious.

"If Char's up for it."

I gave Charlotte my full attention. She shrugged with a soft smile, the questioning look in her eyes gone. "Sure, if there's extra cherries for our sundaes."

"I'll bring a whole jar of maraschinos just for you," I declared. "It's a date. See you both at six." I spun on my heel and went back to work before either could change their minds or argue with the word I'd used.

Just like old times, but I planned on creating something new, hopefully something that would last. No more broken hearts, no more selflessness and setting aside each other's wants. We could have more.

I just needed to convince them.

25

CHARLOTTE

I sat on an old rocking chair, Trina on my lap. She snuggled in close with Lambey and her blanket, thumb in her mouth, the exhaustion of the day pulling on her little eyelids. Being the one to offer comfort, a motherly hold, filled places inside my soul I hadn't known existed. My love for Trina bounded far beyond what I'd expected, and I hugged her closer for it.

The nurse had said the concussion wasn't bad, but she suggested waking Trina every few hours to check on her.

Nathan sat on the couch facing us, his focus solely on his little pumpkin. Dark eyes full of warmth and concern and brow still slightly furrowed, Nathan emitted the kind of protective nature that flipped the on switch for ovaries explode mode. Longing to be with him again clutched at my heart and dug its claws in.

But Liam.

Admitting my want for Nathan didn't diminish my desire for our friend, and although I'd made up my mind, my heart continued to ache for him.

"What are you thinking about?" Nathan's deep voice pulled me from my musings, but sharing the full truth with him might ruin our chances.

"About you."

"What about me?"

"I'm thinking Trina is one very lucky girl to have you in her life. You're a good father figure, Nathan. So unselfish and loving." My smile grew, even though my eyes stung. *And I love you. God, how I love you.*

He inhaled deeply and sat back, hands on his thighs as he studied my face.

Could he see my emotion toward him in my eyes? I'd never been able to hide anything from him. Surely, he must know.

The rocking chair glided smoothly on the hard-wood floor, no squeaks to fill the quietness between us. A moment passed where our gazes connected in silent communication. Shared concern for Trina or perhaps shared memories from our one night together, if the growing desire in his eyes and rising tension in the room was any indicator.

Needing to know, I opened my mouth to ask what he was thinking about, but the flash of head-lights danced across the wall behind him.

"He's here," he said, our time alone ended.

I nodded, turning my focus on Trina as Nathan got up to let him in.

Liam walked into the house like a breath of sunshine, blue eyes lit with happiness, his chatter filling up the heaviness he'd interrupted.

Confusion rose once more to choke the decision I'd made rather than annoyance over his arrival ruining our moment.

Liam had pushed me into changing my mind about Nathan but then invited himself to join us, talking about old times when I'd thought the two of them had a falling out of sorts.

I caught Liam's flirty glances at Nathan while setting down the pizza and a six-pack of beer in the kitchen, his hand and fingertips lingering on Nathan's forearm. Their murmurs didn't reach my ears where I still sat with Trina at the living room's far end.

Nathan stepped closer into his personal space,

and I swore a shiver of electrical energy raised the hairs on my arms. Head tipped back, Liam peered up at Nathan.

Lost in their own world…

Liam had lied, I realized in that moment—and my body loved the thrill of seeing them so close, a breath away from combusting with their desire.

I didn't doubt either's love for one another.

I couldn't deny my own either. I adored my friends in equal measure, and my blood warmed for both, regardless of sexual orientation. I would have given every penny I owned to have Cupid morph the two men into one.

They finally separated, and Liam came into the living room, his cheeks flushed, while Nathan put the box of ice cream into the freezer and retrieved plates from the cabinet.

"How's she doing?" Liam whispered, bending down to check her out.

His cologne filled the air, and even though it wasn't the old Liam scent, I found I'd come to enjoy it all the same, wanting to rub my nose all over his neck. His lips parted with a soft smile, sending a pang through my chest.

When Nathan had pulled him against us in the ER, the brush of Liam's hand against my breast had brought back memories of making out with him. My nipples had hardened, aching for more—so I'd stepped back, the unrest in my mind over the entire situation once more rising.

Emotional attachment to him, the desire to kiss his soft lips wouldn't fade with time. If I decided on Nathan, part of me would always belong to Liam.

I glanced beyond him to find Nathan watching us.

What a mess. What an absolute beautiful mess.

"What?" Liam whispered, tucking my hair behind my ear, his gaze full of the same longing I felt for him in my breast.

"Nothing."

He raised an eyebrow, letting me know he didn't believe me, and my stomach growled.

"We need to feed our woman," he said with a chuckle, turning toward Nathan.

Our woman.

I blinked at the stare Nathan set on Liam's face, the lust in his eyes, the glint of calculation. "What are you up to, Liam?" Nathan asked.

"Eat first. Chat later," Liam replied with a breathless laugh.

My insides fluttered, my skin feeling as though a cool breeze slid over me. Realizing my pulse thrummed louder than my stomach complained, I stood, ignoring the heat of stares on my backside and took Trina to her bedroom.

She blinked sleepily up at me as I tucked her in, and I pressed a kiss to her cheek, my lips lingering as pure joy over taking care of her filled my heart. "Love you, sweet girl."

Without a peep, she closed her eyes, and I slipped out, leaving the door slightly cracked open like Nathan preferred.

I found the men sitting in the living room, Nathan on the couch and Liam in my rocking chair. Garlic and oregano spiciness filled my nose, and I helped myself to two slices of pizza from the box on the coffee table.

"You stole my seat," I told Liam.

"Sit with Nathan. I like looking at the two of you together."

I eyed him while planting my backside where I'd wanted to be anyway. Smirking, he glanced between us, his usual jollity firmly in place. Liam Headley was up to something—and I couldn't quite place my finger on what cooked in his brilliant mind. Whatever it was heightened my pulse and kept me perched on the couch's edge.

"Spill whatever's on your mind, Liam." Nathan

said what I'd been about to.

His eyes widened in feigned innocence. "I'm that transparent?"

"Yes," Nathan and I stated at the same time without hesitation.

Liam laughed, and I shoved pizza into my mouth to give me something to focus on other than the butterflies tickling every inch of my skin.

"Mmm." I closed my eyes at the explosion of flavor on my tongue and slowly chewed, not realizing how hungry I'd been. I hadn't eaten lunch, and we'd been at the hospital for most of the afternoon. Getting discharged always took longer than necessary. It was no wonder my stomach grumbled.

Opening my eyes to check out my next bite, I found both men staring at me. "What?"

"I like watching you eat," Nathan said, his gaze on my mouth.

I glanced at Liam.

He, too, peered at my lips.

My pulse picked back up its rhythm, and I swallowed a rush of saliva that wasn't from the pizza in my hand. "Would you two stop looking at me like *I'm* the pizza, please? It's really...weird." Face heating from my breathless tone, I tore into my slice, chewing loudly with the worst manners possible to make them look elsewhere.

Their continued scrutiny while we all ate near killed me and ruined my panties. I shifted to relieve a growing ache between my thighs.

Liam chuckled at the lust-filled silence hanging over the room, and I scowled.

"What?" I snipped, my thoughts and emotions messier than my first grade classroom after free time.

"I want to know what was going through your mind while watching me and Nathan in the kitchen."

"When?" I said around a mouthful of food, too worked up to care about proper etiquette while eating.

"When I first got here, stepped all up in his personal space, and he didn't back off."

Nathan shifted, pulling my attention away from Liam's twinkling blue eyes half-hidden behind his glasses. He set aside his empty plate, crossing his arms over his chest.

"I was thinking that the two of you look good together." I went for honesty since I couldn't make sense of the hormonal mess in my mind. "Your attraction, your love is so potent it raised the hairs on my arms."

Liam's smirk returned. "What else?"

"What else?" I asked him while glancing at Nathan, so confused by our friend's actions, his words the previous few days, that *lie*, I didn't know what to think.

"Were you turned on?"

I jerked my head toward Liam, pressing my thighs together and hating how well he read me. My face heated. "Um…what?" So much for honesty.

Liam leaned forward, set his plate on the coffee table, and placed his elbows on his knees. "Whatever you felt that gave you goosebumps, did it make you wet?"

"Liam!" Heat flooded through me as all thoughts of finishing my pizza went flying right out the door.

Nathan stared at me, his own face expressionless.

Liam's study of me didn't waver. "Answer the question, Char."

Gaze flitting between the two men, my mouth working like a guppy, I shifted again. Nathan's eyes took on a heated, hooded stare I recognized. Wet didn't begin to describe my panties. "Um…yes?" I choked out.

"Are you thinking what I'm thinking?" Liam asked Nathan, and those piercing eyes turned his way, thank goodness.

"Where's that mind of yours going, Liam?" Nathan's voice hinted at caution in wanting to know the truth of our carefree friend's thoughts.

"The three of us have been on a collision course since we were fifteen," Liam stated with surety. "Our love for one another can't be bound by society's norms. I love you both more than anything on this damn planet, and that's saying something because I love my scalpels and saving lives."

A light bulb shot to life inside my head, and I gasped at what he meant. My gaze flitted between the two men as my stomach fluttered along with my pulse. "Y-You're suggesting the three of us…"

"Yes." No hesitation in Liam's answer, but he turned toward Nathan as I sagged against the couch, mind officially blown. Panties beyond ruined. "You've always been our leader, our true north. I know you want me. I know you want Charlotte. And our poor woman can't hide her need for both of us."

I stared, dumbfounded, my thighs pressed tightly together. *Am* I *that transparent?*

"What do you say, Nathan?" Liam held his gaze as I nodded my easily-won consent. Who needed Cupid when you had Liam?

"Up for a threesome?" he pressed the man we

both loved. "See if we can't figure out this three-way mess of emotions, longing, and lust?"

26

NATHAN

Fuck.

Liam had to go and throw it out there, what I'd been subconsciously thinking about for too damn long, and every muscle in my body clenched in readiness. My brain knew better though.

We'd been friends almost all our lives. Even distance and time hadn't been able to separate or tear apart our connection, but what he suggested could only end in heartache. We'd have to choose at one point, and one of us would end up left behind, broken.

No one could deny the attraction, the love we all felt for each other.

But I hesitated—because of that love.

Things had gone left unsaid, secrets I'd carried with me when I'd taken off all those years ago.

I filled my lungs, steadying myself for the possible shit storm I planned to stir, knowing it could very well put the situation I found myself in to full rest.

Liam knew the truth, but Charlotte didn't.

Unable to watch them both at the same time, I turned my attention on my hands sprawled out on my thighs. The muscles tensed beneath, but I forced my legs to relax.

"I took off for college the way I did because I'd slept with you both and couldn't choose who I wanted to be with. Guilt and fear of breaking someone's heart lit the fire under my ass. Had nothing to do with either of you but my own damn indecision. My inability to make up my mind."

"You don't have to choose now," Liam stated quietly, and I glanced up at Charlotte, needing to see her reaction.

Her gaze flitted between the two of us as she sat back against the couch, her breath seeming to leave in a rush. Her hands clutched the sides of her plate. "You two were having sex."

"Damn near every night," I admitted, even though she hadn't asked a question.

"For how long?"

"Months."

"How did I not know? *Why* didn't I know?"

"Because I'd figured out you liked me as more than a friend, and I didn't want to hurt you."

"I-I can't believe this." She shook her head, fumbling the plate and almost sliding the half piece of pizza onto her lap. "I mean, I'm not angry—or hurt in that way—but… Shit."

My guts twisted over her reaction, but Liam chuckled over the rare curse on her lips. "Are you wet, Char?" he asked.

"Liam!" Her face shaded pink again, and she wouldn't look at either of us.

"That's a yes," Liam said, grinning. "So, what do you say, Nathan? Char? Up for a little tumble in the hay together? Bring to fruition what's been growing beneath the surface for over twenty years? Say the word, and I'm beneath you, between you—however the hell you want me."

Neither of us spoke, but Charlotte's answer shone in her wide, dark eyes, causing my dick to stiffen. To have her between us, sharing in pleasure, fulfilling the lust I'd felt for both as long as I could remember…

Fuck.

The adjustment of my hard-on didn't go unnoticed by either of them.

But I had responsibilities neither of them did, namely a little girl who I was determined to put first in my life. What he suggested would be more than just sex. Could I open myself to vulnerability? The chance of loving and losing? My mom had been torn from my life, the only one who'd ever shown me love, the only one I'd been able to call mine—I couldn't survive that kind of loss again.

It'd left me broken. Empty and angry at the world.

"Our reluctant lumberjack," Liam murmured. "Bet we could talk you into it."

Yeah, I didn't doubt it, which was why I held up my hand when he shifted on his chair like he had ideas of making himself comfy between my legs with those long surgeon fingers and hot mouth.

I didn't want to say no, but I couldn't say yes.

"I need time," I stated quietly, keeping my hand—Liam—in place. "And you both need to fully consider what Liam's suggesting. What Charlotte is salivating for."

Her face turned a deeper shade of red, her nipples hard points.

"Fuck knows, the idea of having you both,

watching you together…Charlotte taking us both inside her turns me the fuck on." My dick leaked inside my jeans, but I ignored the throb in my balls. "But this is more than just sex. There's a little girl to think about. What people would say, how they would react."

Liam wanted to spout off that he didn't give a shit what people would think—I could see it on his face, but he, too, hesitated.

"Trina is my world, and I'm not sure I'm ready to bring in any complications on top of what I'm dealing with right now."

We sat in silence for a few moments, me waiting while they worked through my voiced thoughts. I could see Liam's acceptance first, his smirk emerging.

"Okay." He slapped his thighs and hopped up, heading for the kitchen and one of the bags he'd bought. "Who's ready for ice cream and a movie?"

My breath left in a rush, and Charlotte's resulting smile wobbled. "Can we still snuggle?" she asked.

"Finish your pizza then get your fine ass over here," I growled at her.

Her light laughter, shaky with nervousness, filled my chest with warmth.

Liam sauntered back into the living room and

fumbled with my old DVD player, his backside tucked tightly into a pair of skinny jeans.

Fuck. Adjusting myself again, I cursed my life. What man wanted to bone both his best friends in equal measure?

Me. That's who.

Scowling, I grabbed the last piece of pizza out of the box to keep my hands occupied and steeled myself for temptation of the worst kind.

27
LIAM

Days passed, and agitation set me on edge.

I'd talked to Charlotte twice in the week since I had laid out my plan and set my heart on a platter for my two best friends to stab with forks, but she dismissed my ideas on how to seduce Nathan.

She hopped aboard my suggestion of the three of us together though, even admitting she'd wished me and Nathan could morph into a single man. But she, too, wanted to think of Trina first.

I felt like a selfish bastard, but I followed Nathan's lead, same as always.

It would be up to him to make the first move. I just hoped his reluctance wore thin before I lost my damn mind. While at work, I thought of him.

Her.

Us.

At least I managed to wield my scalpels with precision, my decisions solid, all thoughts of lust and longing set aside while in surgery. But after seven days of silence, something had to give.

I ached for my sweet Charlotte, and I needed my reluctant lumberjack to yield to what I knew had been meant to be from the day we'd all drawn our first breaths. Never had I been so sure of something in my life.

Friday afternoon, my final surgery of the day wrapped up and in recovery, I headed out of the doctor's lounge, intent on getting the ball rolling. I just hadn't figured out what. Show up at Nathan's house and make him admit what he wanted? Finally lose myself in Charlotte and talk her into seducing him together?

Or head to Mel's and get a burger, a couple beers, and just enjoy some *me* downtime. Fuck knew I could use that too.

"Help me!" a man bellowed, and I instinctively jerked around toward the ER entrance at the end of the hallway behind me.

Billy Jenkins.

Bloodied and stumbling—carrying a limp woman whose intestines spilled from her stomach.

I barked out orders to the ER nurses while sprinting his way.

"Don't touch my fuckin' wife!" Billy screamed the second he saw me, yanking her body tight against his chest. "Don't need no fuckin' fag putting his hands on her!"

I stepped back rather than argue, allowing a nurse and Doctor Lynch to get up close and assess. Billy's wife had been ripped into. Wild animal? Rabid dog? Whatever had gotten to her stomach cavity had done serious damage, the kind that would have gotten my ass called back to the hospital even if I'd been gone for the day.

I headed back the way I'd come. Billy's wife would be under lights and anesthesia within a matter of minutes while he remained in the waiting room. He wouldn't know who performed surgery until it was too late, and while I would love to hurt him the same way he'd hurt me for all those years in our childhood, I'd become a better man.

A man who'd taken an oath to save lives, and nothing and no one would keep me from doing my job.

Mind set on what I could control, I focused on the truth and went to work.

28

CHARLOTTE

With school out for the summer and nothing to keep me occupied, I read like a hungry cat, stalking my next book boyfriend and lounging with everyone I found between the pages. Devouring words, made-up love stories, kept my mind occupied while Nathan decided what he wanted.

If my e-reader's to-read list was any indication, I was on board. With bells on.

Menage titles littered my home page, and every single one a male-on-male-on-female, the newest, Healing Storms, making me cry and then heating me up. Jill, the female lead, lucked out by falling for two men who secretly loved one another. And when the poopy hit the fan, they recognized their love and found happiness.

The best part of their story? I gained a few new fantasies.

My vibrator got a workout, and I probably put on a few pounds from not moving off my couch. The only time I spent in the real world was when Mom or Liam buzzed my cell.

He baited and tempted me into helping him sway Nathan our way, his pleadings intensifying with every call. By day four, he sounded like an agitated blue jay, and on day five, he revisited that simple gift he'd offered weeks earlier.

His need influenced my own, until I, too, reached a breaking point.

But I didn't wield a sharp instrument, holding people's lives in my hands, like he did.

While I'd texted Nathan a few times during the week to check on Trina, I broke down and made a call on day seven, my pulse rapid to the point my fingers shook while tapping his name on my cell.

His breathless, deep hello hardened my nipples to points.

Butterflies took to flight in my belly. "Hey. Bad time?"

"No. Just splitting wood."

I imagined his unbuttoned flannel, the hair spattered over thick pecs I wanted to trail my fingertips across. My mouth watered. "H-How's Trina?" I sputtered, clenching my thighs together.

"She's good," he grunted as though annoyed. "Bored and driving me insane with her whining."

I couldn't help my laugh, having the perfect opportunity. "Sounds like you need another break."

"Yeah."

"Is Agatha around?"

"It's Friday."

"Oh. Gossip Girl night." I considered all of three seconds before blurting, "I could always stop by."

"I'd like that."

His rumbled reply hinted at wanting more than a break, and I hopped off my couch faster than I had all week.

"I'll swing by in an hour," I said, while hurrying toward the bathroom for a good shower and thorough shave, leaving remnants of my afternoon laying where I'd dropped them. Emptied bag of chips. Candy wrapper. Bowl with dried smears of the ice cream I'd had for lunch. "Want me to grab something for dinner?"

"Trina!" he called. "You want chicken nuggies and fries for supper?"

Her squeal answered, and his chuckle in my ear

sent all kinds of delicious shivers over my heated skin.

"Chicken nuggies, it is," I said. I got his order and hung up, letting out a similar squeal to Trina's.

I SHOWED up at the Oakland homestead to find Nathan showered, dressed in a tight t-shirt, beard trimmed, and hot gaze plastered on me as I climbed from my car.

"You look good enough to eat." His low, quiet tone caressed all my erogenous zones like a whisper, raising the hairs on my arms as I handed over the bags of fast food. "Tell me you're bare under that sundress."

"I'm bare under my sundress," I admitted like a breathless slut, ready to drop and spread my legs at his command.

Nathan's groan pulsed through my core. "Christ." He spun and made for the house. "Come on in. Trina's in the living room."

Letting out a slow trickled exhale through my parted lips, I followed on his heels, everything about his broad back, the narrow waist, and tree-trunk thighs a temptation. Memories stole my mind of his big hands on me, his weight pressing me into my parents' couch, his girth stretching me to the point I'd cried tears he'd licked from my cheeks.

I'd lived in fear those first six weeks afterwards due to a late period, even though he'd used a condom. Eventually, I'd gotten my period, and I assumed the stress over his disappearance and Liam's heartbreak atop mine had messed with my hormones.

Funny how I'd been so scared of being pregnant back then but longed for it more than anything now.

Trina squealed as I walked into the house, launching herself into my arms and completely melting my heart.

"Someone is back to normal," I said with a laugh and smooched her cheeks until she wiggled to get down. "No more boo boos?" I asked with a quick glance at the stitches on her forehead.

"Chicken nuggies!" She bolted to her chair at the kitchen table rather than answering me, and I settled in beside her, passing out napkins from the holder at the table's center.

Trina chatted while we ate, keeping the tension between Nathan and me to a minimum. But once we finished, got her washed up of ketchup smears, and Nathan sprawled on the couch, watching her and I play dolls on the floor, the longing, the discomfort of too much need swirling inside me returned.

Legs spread and arm across the couch's back, Nathan remained focused on us. Stared with hooded eyes and not at his little ward.

With my girls squashed into the top of my sundress, I may have bent here and there a little deeper than necessary, offering him an eyeful of cleavage.

He shifted and adjusted himself a few times, creating a furnace inside me over the fact I turned him on, same as I did Liam. Me. The one who couldn't find a decent date. I aroused both of the men of my dreams.

"You're going to be an incredible mother," he murmured out of the blue, snagging my full attention off the fake bottle I held to my assigned doll's mouth.

"I tried three times to get pregnant," I blurted, my face heating over the instant scowl denting his eyebrow.

"What?" he all but growled.

"Well, I couldn't get a date, couldn't find a man." I fumbled with the bottle, and Trina took it from me, intending to feed the doll herself. "The two men I'd always wanted had taken off, so I decided on artificial insemination," I pretty much whispered, unable to look at him to see his reaction to the loss I couldn't escape.

He didn't respond, and I eventually glanced up to find his brow smoothed as he studied me.

"I was desperate," I said with a shrug, my smile wobbly.

"It didn't work."

"No." While the lack of life growing in my belly hit me with grief like a truck every time the truth resurfaced, I wondered if fate hadn't intended things to work out the way they had.

He offered no pity. Simply stared at me until the feelings of loss faded into the tension that rose between us like it always did whenever we locked eyes. Urgency to touch him, kiss him, and hold him, skin on skin, rose inside me

"Dolly has a poopy diapew," Trina announced, pulling us both from our bubble of desire, me chuckling over her word choice.

"Bath time," Nathan rumbled, and although Trina whined, he got her in the tub while I retrieved the bottle of wine I'd brought along, just in case he invited me to stick around.

He did.

I sipped my Riesling, listening to Nathan hum

silly songs to Trina while she splashed in the tub. He'd claimed I would make a good mother, but did he know how much he excelled at loving that little girl? Did he recognize what a gift he'd become to Trina, and how his tender, protective actions with her would make me fall harder for him?

She made him laugh as the water drained. She also demanded Charlotte's Web before bedtime, giving me more time with my thoughts on love, longing, and the passing of time.

With the longer summer days, the sunset still lit the sky when he laid her down for the night, and my nervousness over being alone with him beat out the slight buzz the wine gifted me. I sat curled on the couch, not too far into one corner but not so close to the middle that he would sit in the chair.

I had no plans to seduce. No ideas to attempt what I'd done once before, but I couldn't keep my mind from wishing for that very thing.

The light switched off in Trina's bedroom. Nathan's, "Goodnight, pumpkin," reached my ears, and I took another big gulp of wine to steady my shaking hands.

29

NATHAN

Charlotte had to go and tell me a thing like that. Trying to get pregnant out of desperation through medical means and having endured all she'd gone through made me half-sick. Had I known, had I kept in touch, artificial insemination wouldn't have been on the table.

Yeah, things would have been different, but I couldn't dwell on the what-ifs.

Imagining Charlotte growing round with my child though—*that* was some shit worth thinking on. Made my dick like fucking rock. Ready to bust and shoot what she needed deep inside her lush body.

I didn't let Trina linger in the tub. Kept the reading to one chapter rather than drone on until she passed out. My heart beat heavy in my chest as I pulled her door mostly shut and strode back to the living room to Charlotte who was desperate for my dick beyond the required sperm she needed to get pregnant.

She was too guilt-ridden to try to seduce me again, but what she lusted after heated her eyes, tightened her nipples to hard points, and pulsed through the artery in her neck.

Charlotte sat on my couch in her red-flowered sundress, her bare feet tucked beneath her. She wore no panties—fuck, the thought of her wet warmth and the need in her eyes as she watched me draw closer…I wanted it.

Her.

A child.

Fuck, I wanted it *all* like a greedy, selfish bastard.

I'd denied us twenty years of what could have been heaven, all out of fear. She'd fit me perfectly, same as Liam had, and I'd never found someone to replace either of them. Putting aside thoughts of regret, I approached the couch, standing over her rather than sitting.

She peered up at me with her luminous dark eyes in the lamp's light, and I bent down, hands on the back of the couch on either side of her head, putting my face inches from hers. Breath caught, she peered up at me.

"You deserve to be a mother," I told her the truth I felt in my soul, "and I desperately want to give you that."

"I-I'm not ovulating right now."

"Don't give a shit. Still want to try. I need to see if you're half as perfect as I remember. If you taste as sweet, if your pussy sucks me in like it can't get enough. See if all my filthy fantasies live up to reality."

Her pupils dilated, lips parted. "Filthy?" she whispered, her voice raw with desire.

"I'm going to spread you open. Tongue your holes. Breathe in your musk. Taste your cream and lap it up until I can't think beyond you—your sweetness, your essence. *You*. I'm going to lose myself in you and not come up for air until I'm gasping for my last breath."

Charlotte pressed a fingertip to my lips, and I held still, fighting off my body's tremble.

This woman...

"Yes," she whispered. "A thousand times, yes."

A mere touch, a whisper of breath fanned over my face, and I wanted to bury myself inside her and die a contented man. I'd felt the same with Liam, and while I didn't understand why the draw between the three of us was so strong or what we should do about it, I couldn't deny myself or Charlotte any longer.

I leaned in, and she gave me her mouth with a whimper that tightened my balls up against my groin. So much softer than Liam's mouth, but no less hungry, she returned my kiss, grasping at my beard to pull me closer.

Without looking, she set her wine glass aside and yanked on my shirt as though desperate to touch hot skin. Her hands mapped the contours beneath my shirt, her fingertips dancing down my abs, contracting the muscle beneath and rushing fire through my blood.

Falling to my knees, I tugged her closer to the couch's edge, grabbed hold of her hair, and sank into her mouth, licking and biting, our tongues fucking. Tasting.

Charlotte deserved to be spread out and devoured, not fucked on a narrow couch we both wouldn't fit on.

"Char," I groaned, both of my hands on her face, holding her still for me to catch my breath.

"I ache to feel you. Inside me, no barriers."

Her words rushed hot need through me, and I groaned, tipping my forehead against hers.

"I was selfish once upon a time, and I want more now. Wreck me, Nathan. Shatter my memories and make new ones."

Zero fucking reluctance hindered my thought process. I stood, pulling her to her feet without a word. She shivered as I laced my fingers through hers and led her back through the hallway. After a quick, silent shut of Trina's door, I tugged Charlotte into my room.

My queen-sized bed barely fit me, but we'd make do.

I left the lights on. Stared into her widened eyes while stripping her down. Ran my hands over her front, mapping out her curves, the extra flesh she'd always hated that filled my hands with satiny softness I wanted to bury myself in.

Dick leaking, I imagined fucking between her huge tits. Her pussy. Her ass. Hell, I even considered fucking her damn armpit—the woman owned my desire and had the body to satisfy my cravings.

I cupped her sex, her dampness coating my palm. "I want all of you."

"You can have it," she whispered, her hands on my chest.

Sliding two fingers deep inside her body brought a gasp to her parted lips. "This is mine."

"What if Liam wants it too?" she asked as I pumped in and out of her.

I groaned at the thought of him taking her, of both of us having her at the same time. "Then I'll share," I declared against her mouth, my fate sealed as our lips did. "Lay back on the bed and let me look at you."

Pink fused through her cheeks and chest while she eased back, hands holding her breasts up.

"Let them go. Open your thighs so I can see what's mine *to share*." Another whimper left her, but she did as I asked.

Pink, wet folds held my stare. Swollen and slick. Her clit protruded beneath her patch of trimmed hair, her hole dark and promising.

I couldn't rip my shirt off fast enough, couldn't push down my jeans without hopping on one foot in my haste.

Charlotte's gaze glued to my raging hard-on as I grabbed hold of my base and stroked upward, smearing the welling pre-cum at the tip down my length.

She fucking wet her lip like she wanted a taste, but I wouldn't last if she put her mouth on me.

I crawled between her spread thighs and rubbed my leaking dick all over her hole, her clit, sliding through the wetness of her pussy to get myself good and slick for what I wanted. "Anyone take you here?" I asked through clenched teeth, sliding my throbbing head over her asshole.

"No." She gasped as I pressed just enough to tease, but I shifted upward.

"You're all mine right now."

Although Char trembled, she relaxed—and I slid fucking home into her pussy with one slow glide, rather than having to work to shove my way inside inch by inch like the first time I'd fucked her. I lowered my body over hers, claiming her mouth as I bottomed out against her womb.

She tasted better than I remembered, her sheath tighter, hotter than my fantasies. The softness of her around me, the feminine curves welcoming me— fucking heaven.

I couldn't hold still any longer.

My balls throbbed, and our combined groans as I pulled out and sank back into her lush body took me to the brink of blowing in seconds.

Seated deep, I held still again and focused on the tartness of wine on her tongue, the tremors rippling through her body beneath mine. Her hands clutching at me, her thighs cradling my body.

"Like a goddamn glove, Char," I murmured against her mouth, nipping her lower lip. "So fucking perfect for me. Christ."

Planking, I backed out, watching my glistening dick slide out of her grasp. Her fingernails clutched at my shoulders, her heels digging into my ass to keep me from retreating fully.

"Nathan," she whimpered as I left her empty except for the head of my dick, barely notched.

"This what you want?" I asked, holding her hot stare while pushing back in, bumping her womb again.

"Yes." Her back arched. "Oh, fuck, yes."

"My sweet Char—what a potty mouth you've got." I chuckled, drawing out and shoving back in with a quicker snap of my hips. "I never knew."

"It's you."

I thrust again.

"Fuck, it's you," she whispered, her head tipping back, lips left parted. "All you."

A swivel of my hips rubbed my pelvis over her clit, and she shuddered.

"Again."

I gave her what she wanted, thrusting and

grinding until red splotches covered her cheeks and bouncing breasts.

"Fucking gorgeous." I buried my face in the soft flesh of her tits, biting and sucking, breathing her in. Never enough—I wouldn't ever get my fill of her.

I swiveled my hips, grinding against her clit, thrusting and groaning over her gasps.

Rising once more onto my hands, I snagged her hazed stare. "Tell me what you want, Char. Tell me how you need me to move—how you've dreamed about me fucking you."

"H-harder," she whispered with another shudder. She panted, her eyes lost to lust.

I let loose, the knowledge I didn't have to hold back for fear of hurting her so fucking freeing I wanted to explode. I spread her open, leg over my shoulder, and pounded into her.

"Like this, Char? Hmm?" I jabbed deep, every whimper and gasp from her swollen lips egging me on. "I want you to come all over my dick, Char, then I'm going to fill you up."

"Yes."

Her back slid along the mattress as I slammed into her over and over. "You're going to take every drop, hold it inside your greedy little pussy."

"Oh..." She let out a low whine, her pussy

clamping down on my thrusting length. "Nathan—" Her voice caught on a gasp, and I collapsed down atop her, taking her mouth, fucking into her with abandon. I chased release with her while swallowing her cries.

Three thrusts, and I erupted, cum spurting deep as it could go, every pulse of her pussy around my length demanding I give her more.

I gave her everything. Every drop in my aching balls. Every piece of my heart—save one.

The part of me that Liam owned.

In that moment, I knew where my heart belonged, in whose hold. Three precious souls held my happiness in their hands, two being my lovers. I wanted them both with an intensity that scared the shit out of me, and since I couldn't choose, I decided I would have what my heart longed for, just like Liam had suggested.

Rest finally swept into my head, settling my thoughts, and with a final grunt, I went lax against Char's soft body, my face buried in her neck.

The chips could fall where they would, and I would be there to protect all three from the backlash.

I saved Billy Jenkin's wife. Four hours of hell, touch and go. The woman was lucky to be breathing, but she had a long road to recovery ahead of her. As the surgeon, it hadn't just been my job to keep her alive but to talk to the family afterward. That part scared me more than putting her intestines back together and tucked away where they belonged.

Armpits prickling, I swallowed hard and pushed through the door into the waiting area.

Billy and his wife's parents sat alone in the waiting room, and while he scowled, the parents hopped up, hurrying toward me.

I smiled my joy at keeping her alive a little while longer, and Billy sank back against his chair—still frowning but keeping his thoughts about me to himself while I shared the outcome of the surgery.

Her mother cried, her father holding her while thanking me.

Billy rubbed a hand down over his weary face, his dented brow relaxing at my encouragement. He met my gaze and nodded a single time.

No verbal offer of thanks or a handshake, but since I'd expected more heated words or a possible black eye for touching his property, elation swept over me.

"She has a long road ahead of her, but I think she's going to be just fine," I told him.

A muscle twitched in his jaw, but he nodded again.

I left them alone, my throat tight.

The second I made it into the doctor's lounge, I hissed a few excited curses, my footsteps light while gathering my shit to go home. I couldn't wait to tell Charlotte, but more, I couldn't wait to see the look on Nathan's face when I told him that Billy had acted like an adult around me. Acknowledged me beyond the usual curses of being a low-life faggot who deserved death.

Rather than head home, I took a quick shower in the lounge, grinning like an ass the entire time.

Within minutes, I flew up the road toward the opposite side of town, more butterflies in my stomach than had been there while I'd scrubbed for surgery. I gunned it up Nathan's driveway, my smile widening when I saw Charlotte's car alongside his truck.

I hopped from my car, sprinting on air while hurrying to his front door. A quick knock, and I actually fucking giggled, shoving my hands in my jeans' pockets to keep them from shaking.

The door pulled open.

Nathan was shirtless and sweaty, his jeans unbuttoned and open enough to give me an eyeful of dark hair and the root of his dick. Wetness smeared over his groin—he smelled of sex.

My dick shot to full attention, and I adjusted myself with a groan while forcing my focus upward. "Can I come?" A laugh burst from me. "Come in, I mean."

Nathan's crooked smirk twitched his beard, and he stepped back, allowing me entry, no trace of guilt or unease on his face or in his stance. He didn't mind I'd all but caught him and Char fucking.

His dark eyes twinkled a bit, as if pleased I'd shown up when I had.

"Where is she?" I asked, glancing into the empty living room.

"In my bed."

Damn. She lay in his bed—and he seemed happy to see me. I could only imagine if Char would look as wrecked as I'd felt when Nathan had fucked me.

I strode back the hallway to find out, knowing he would follow on my heels, and my heart beat faster for it. Anticipation swirled inside me, but I pushed down expectations over what the night might hold. Disappointment never went well for my needy ass.

Trina's door closed fully…he'd meant business.

I couldn't help my heightened giddiness, and my knees actually went weak.

Low light shone like a beacon into the hallway from the other bedroom door, and the second I crossed the threshold into Nathan's bedroom, my gaze latched onto Charlotte's red face.

Sated. Yet embarrassed. Freshly fucked and beyond beautiful.

"Liam," she whispered, clutching the sheet up to her neck, her gaze flitting to Nathan whose heated presence tingled my backside as the door clicked shut and locked behind me.

"Fancy finding you right where I want to be," I said with a smile.

"I'm—well, I didn't mean for, well, that is to say—"

"Shh," I shushed Char, moving closer to sit on the bed's edge beside her while trying to control my inner tremors. "You'll never guess who came into the ER tonight."

She blinked at my change of topic, and Nathan stayed three feet away, hands fisted at his sides like he held back from ripping into me like he'd obviously done to her.

My dick jerked inside my pants, but I focused on the story I had to tell. We'd get to satisfying his lust along with mine—I hoped. "Billy Jenkins."

"Fucker," Nathan muttered.

"His wife was ripped into by a dog. Guts spilling out and everything."

Charlotte grimaced and shook her head. "No details, sicko."

"Pansy." I grinned. "Even though he hollered at me not to touch her when they first came in, I saved her life. And afterward? He nodded his thanks. No screaming, no fists. He actually acknowledged what I'd done."

"Well, fuck me."

My dick wept inside my jeans at Nathan's curse.

"Gladly," I said like a breathless whore, winking up at him.

He studied me with an intensity in his dark eyes that curled my toes and clenched my asshole. "You've always been so cautious, Liam. Thinking shit through before acting. You sure about this?" he asked, motioning at Char, at me, at himself.

Hell, yes, and then some. My blood ran hot at the thought. "Are *you*?"

"I want you both. No fucking denying that, and I'm tired of fighting it. Tired of living without you. Both of you. Yes, I want this—so tell me, yes or no, because I need a definite answer."

"Yes." A simple reply, the one he obviously hoped for.

He shoved down his jeans, kicking them aside, and I zoned in on the semi between his powerful thighs, still wet and sticky from their fucking. Saliva pooled in my mouth, and I set my glasses on the bed stand and slid off the mattress, dropping to my knees to take what I wanted.

31

CHARLOTTE

Merciful Lord in heaven...

My breath caught, my core throbbing at the sight of Liam sucking Nathan's length into his mouth. Fantasy one of a million thoroughly fulfilled.

Nathan groaned and grabbed hold of Liam's hair, pulling his face flush against his groin. A few muttered curses escaped his parted lips, and Liam hummed his approval while backing off, his tongue swirling around Nathan's swollen head as though lapping at every trace of our combined cum. What should have sickened me turned me on faster and stronger than any kiss, any touch.

"She likes watching us," Nathan said with a grunt, yanking Liam close again. "Is your pussy needy, Char? Wet and feeling empty?"

"Yes," I answered, even though heat flooded my face with the honesty of my body's reaction over seeing them together.

"Enough." Nathan pushed Liam off him, his mouth releasing with a pop that tightened my core.

"So hot," I whispered, fisting the sheet beneath my chin to keep from reaching between my thighs.

Hard shaft still in hand, Nathan moved across the room toward his dresser.

"Baby monitor?" Liam asked as Nathan flicked it on.

"I knew you and Char would end up in my bed eventually," Nathan said, stalking our way again, "and I'm not fucking either of you without closed and locked doors. I plan on taking you both, but make no mistake—she calls, I'm done. Whether I'm balls deep or down your throat, if Trina needs me, I'm stepping out."

"Aaand my ovaries just exploded," I whispered, pressing my thighs tight while Liam chuckled.

Nathan settled on the bed, leaning against the headboard beside me, slowly jacking himself. "Do you want Liam, Char?" he asked, serious as I'd ever heard him. "Want to be the first—and only—pussy Liam will ever have?"

"Yes," I didn't hesitate, my gaze captured by

Liam's pupil-blown blues. "You can take whatever you want, Liam," I said, my voice shaking as quickly as my insides fluttered. "I'm yours. Both of yours."

"Give me something to jerk off to," Nathan said with a grunt.

Liam stripped fast at Nathan's command, his focus not leaving my face. "Let me see you?" His high tenor voice wavered, easing the embarrassment inside me.

I'd loved Liam since childhood. My best friend. He'd been with me at my worst, at my best.

I had nothing to hide.

Pushing down the sheet, I still found myself biting the inside of my lip. Hoping, praying, to find desire in his eyes as he raked his focus down over my nakedness. Large breasts. Extra around my middle. Chubby legs.

Liam's dick jutted straight out, leaking, all while looking at me—not Nathan.

Me.

Fatty, Thick Thigh Charlotte.

I held out my hand, my throat tight, and he crawled up onto the bed, on his haunches between my spread legs. He laced the fingers of one of his hands with mine.

"So pretty," he said, his focus on where I dripped

cum and desperately wanted more, even though I swore Nathan had already tired out my insides.

I expected shame or embarrassment, but neither assaulted me as Liam reached out to touch. Feel. My hips lifted, and I pressed my lips tight to keep from begging for more as he dipped a single finger inside me.

Liam groaned. "So soft…" He pushed in deeper and pulled out, the wet sound heating even the tips of my ears.

"Liam," I whimpered like I hadn't just been fucked harder than I had in my entire life by the mass of man sitting beside me, still working his mouthwatering length.

"I think he likes your pussy," Nathan said, his low rumble tightening my nipples.

"Hell yeah." Liam's quick, rasped agreement caused laughter to flutter through my chest, but I bit it back.

Nerves, need…I felt like a jumble of emotions ready to bubble over.

"Liam," I repeated my plea, tugging on his hand.

He finally tore his focus off my core, those baby blues of his latching onto my face, his slow smile lighting me up from the inside out. "You're my first."

And I thought his touch had made me feel like a

powerful queen. Liam rubbed the back of his hardness along my slick folds, flexing his ass to rub up over my clit.

"Oh… Please, Liam." I shifted my hips beneath him, trying to line him up to fill me. My legs wound around his thighs, my hands finding his tight, little backside. "Please."

The tip of him pressed against me, and he cradled my face in his hands, smoothing back my hair while lowering onto his elbows. "I've always loved you, Char." One slow thrust buried him inside my body, and he kissed me, both of our moans mingling between our fused lips.

He shuddered in my arms, and I clung to him tighter, wanting him deeper, inside my body, my head, my heart.

Not close enough.

Never close enough.

"You feel so good, Char," he groaned against my mouth while dragging his length out of me. "So. Fucking. Good." Three quick thrusts accompanied his words.

Nathan cursed along with an agreement. I glanced up to find his dark eyes hooded and riveted on us, his beard twitching as though he clenched his teeth, the veins in his forearm popping as he continued to work himself. "Watching him fuck you is better than I imagined it'd be."

"Mmm," Liam moaned, pushing up onto his hands to watch his length appear and disappear back inside me. "So good, Char. Goddamn, how have I lived without you all these years? If I'd known..." Liam shook his head and grinned down at me.

If I'd known, I would have pounced on his offer that first night, period be damned. Having Liam inside my body connected us on such a deeper level than we'd experienced, filled me with a headier love and lust than I'd had for him before.

"You're fucking perfect, Char," Liam whispered, his eyelids sliding shut, head hanging enough that his hair tumbled over his forehead. "So soft. So wet —full of Nathan's cum."

Nathan groaned along with me, Liam's words causing even more arousal to rush straight to my core. "Fuck," Nathan cursed lowly as though through clenched teeth.

"Yeah," Liam agreed, moving his hips in circles, rubbing over my clit, his lower lip between his teeth.

Liam had always been handsome in my eyes, but passion-crazed, lust-filled Liam who chewed his lip to death while taking pleasure in my body?

Yeah.

I shivered beneath him, our bodies moving in perfect rhythm, coming together and gliding apart in delicious friction.

He lowered over me again, drawing up his knees to open me wider, and set a steady pace of thrusting, his mouth suddenly turning needy and consuming.

My heart raced, tingles of another climax simmering just beyond reach as I held him close.

"Fuck." Nathan shifted, dipping the bed, and crawled around behind Liam. "I need you."

Liam moaned against my mouth, his hips pulling back, barely keeping the swollen head of him inside my body. He tore his lips from me, panting, tipping down to rest his forehead against mine.

He shuddered as though barely hanging onto his sanity.

"What's he doing?" I asked, just as breathless as him.

"Lubing my hole. Oh, fuck…" Liam's low groan and his arching back shot lust, pure and frantic, through me.

"You like my finger in your ass while her sweet pussy sucks on your dick?" Nathan's words intensified my desire, and I planted my feet on the mattress, lifting my hips in desperation to have Liam fully inside me again.

"Please," I found myself whispering again, need-ing...so much *need.*

With a groan, Liam sank back into my body as though he'd been pushed, his face burying in my neck.

I caught Nathan's focus over his shoulder. He held Liam's lower back firmly with one hand, his other hand rubbing along where Liam and I joined. So much wetness smeared between us, he slid two fingers inside me alongside Liam's length, stretching me until I gasped at the sting.

Liam ground his hips against me, his whispered, "Fuck" against my neck sending shivers over my skin.

Nathan's fingers slid out, but Liam stayed put, trembling.

"Hurry, Nathan," Liam groaned, "or I'm gonna blow."

Dark eyes focused between my thighs, and I longed for a mirror to watch how he touched Liam. "What are you doing?" I had to know.

Liam muttered a curse.

"Stretching his hole to take my dick."

"Oh...oh merciful..." I gulped, my body pulsing tightly around Liam's girth.

"I'm ready—for fuck's sake, Nathan, I'm ready!"

Liam gasped, once more shuddering atop me. He released a rushed exhale.

Nathan shifted forward, and Liam let out a steady, low moan, his body pressing down on mine, his length shoving in a little deeper.

"Oh fuck." Liam hissed against my neck, his teeth nipping.

Nathan's dark stare caught and held my eyes, the steady flexing of his hips moving Liam inside me.

"God…fucking *hell*." Liam groaned. "Holy *fuck*."

"Mmm." Nathan's deep groan sent heat sweeping through me and a rush of wetness around Liam's length.

Dick, Char. You're a true, wanton whore now. Two men in a matter of minutes. And the thought of the sight of the three of us together… Hell, I'd already said fuck in front of Nathan twice.

The two of them had ruined me for life, but I wasn't about to complain.

My toes tingled with the beginnings of a climax, and I moved beneath Liam, shifting with every flex of Nathan's backside. I gladly took what he gave, every grunt and thrust pressing me into the mattress ingrained in my memory.

"Gonna come inside you, Char," Liam rasped out, his fingers tangled in my hair, his face still buried against my throat. "He's going to fuck the cum right out of me—right into you. Fucking hell…"

My breath caught—and I fell, a rush of euphoria sweeping over me. "Yes," I cried out, Nathan's firm thrusts slamming Liam into me, hitting my cervix.

"Char," he groaned, and his dick pulsed deep inside me, coating me with the wet heat of his cum. "Fuck, Char. God*damn*!"

Nathan pounded into Liam from behind, sliding our bodies along the bed. The sound of wet flesh slapping reached through my ringing ears as I came down, and I blinked, desperate to keep Nathan in focus as he found his release.

Head tipped back, his shoulders tensed—I could imagine the sure bruising on Liam's hips from where he held him. Veins bulged in his neck, his forehead, and his lips parted as he emitted rumbling grunts with every thrust.

"Christ!" he whisper-hollered and slammed into Liam. Another smaller climax rippled through my core as Nathan came, his dark eyes hazed over, same as when he'd filled me full of cum.

Liam panted against my neck.

Nathan cursed behind him until stilling.

And me? I smiled, even as tears trickled down my cheeks. Certainly not conventional, but I knew without doubt, we'd come to the place we were meant to be. A tangle of limbs, panting breaths caressing sweaty skin. Thrumming hearts and shuddered sighs.

Together. All three of us.

Nathan leaned over Liam's back and kissed me softly. Tenderly, telling me with a simple brush of his lips that he agreed we'd found what we'd all been searching for.

32

NATHAN

I didn't want to move. Didn't want to pull my semi from Liam's ass, didn't want to stop kissing Charlotte. But Liam whimpered between us, and I backed out slowly, sliding out of his body. His hole gaped, a pulse of white dripping out as the pink, puckered skin closed shut.

"Damn," he muttered from where he still buried his face against Charlotte's softness. "I've always loved your dick, Nathan, but having Charlotte on the other end—fucking perfection."

Charlotte giggled, her eyes still wet with happy tears—I didn't doubt their origin. The love shining from them while I'd abused Liam's hole had pulled me over the edge just as much as his tight heat clamping around my dick.

Sinking back on my haunches, I grabbed hold of his hips, easing him away from our woman.

A rush of wetness came from her core along with his flaccid dick, and I gathered it up with two fingers and pushed it back in as Liam moved off to the side, his arm still over her chest, his sated eyes finding mine.

"Putting our cum back inside her?"

"Damn right," I muttered, rubbing my thumb over the swollen, pink lips to her clit.

She jolted beneath my touch, grasping at my hand to stop me from stimulating her further. "Too much."

I slid my fingers out and back in, the wet squishing sounds almost enough to make my dick hard again.

If I'd been eighteen and not nearly forty.

Liam squeezed her tight with a little sigh deflating him, and I pulled my sopping fingers free from Char.

Wet and sticky… I lifted my hand to my nose and breathed them both in.

Fuck it.

I flicked out my tongue, tasting her—and him.

"Still gay for me?" Liam asked with a grin as I

coated my tongue with a guy's spunk for the first time.

I took my time licking both of my fingers clean before answering, my dick *wishing* to be eighteen again. "Always."

"Still straight for me?" Char asked Liam with another soft laugh that jiggled her gorgeous tits.

"Oh, hell yeah," he said with another sigh, latched onto her side like an insatiable kid. "I'm thoroughly addicted to your pussy."

"Neither of you move," I said, pushing off the bed, my lips twitching at Liam's declaration. He'd never been into pussy. Ever. Same as I'd never wanted dick.

Love—does some fucking strange things to a body, heart, and soul.

My legs had been done in, same as my dick, and I stumbled into the bathroom. Couldn't remember when I'd gotten hard and fucked twice in that short a time.

Not since Liam and I were just kids.

I eyed myself in my bathroom mirror while wetting a couple hand cloths to clean up the two gorgeous people in my bed.

We'd fit together like we belonged. No weirdness, no selfishness. Yeah, I'd lusted after Liam's ass after a few minutes of watching him lose himself in heaven, but he'd wanted it too. Charlotte's blown pupils and panted breaths told me she'd been ready for the three of us to come together.

My needy little lovers.

Beard twitching again in a grin I couldn't hold back, I returned to find them unmoved.

We'd made one hell of a mess on my bed, but I couldn't find two fucks to give. My cum, Liam's cum, Charlotte's cum—nothing had ever satisfied me more than seeing my sheets wet with it. Knowing I'd made the right decision, I cleaned them both up regardless of their objections, settling in on Charlotte's other side once done.

Liam and I scooted in close, squishing her between us, her warm breath fanning my chin, her soft tits pressed against my chest. I kissed her forehead and grabbed Liam's ass, holding him tight.

"I feel like a slice of cheese," Charlotte said with a giggle.

Liam's cheeks moved beneath my palm as he ground against her backside. "I like cheese."

She slapped at his hand sneaking between her and my body with another laugh.

"I like cheese too," I said, not even bothering to

rub on her. Wouldn't be able to get it up again if I wanted to.

"You two are going to be the death of me," Charlotte stated with a laugh.

"We're just getting started," Liam said, with so much damn happiness on his face I couldn't keep from letting my grin out.

33

LIAM

"Well, fuck me," I said with a breathless rush, staring at the grin stretching Nathan's lips. "That smile is lethal, Nathan Oakland."

"So's your tight ass." He squeezed my backside with his meaty paw, holding me against the softest skin I'd ever felt in my life.

A shuddering sigh ripped through me, and I closed my eyes, nuzzling my nose in Char's hair, soaking in every inch of her deliciousness pressing against my front. My insides lit up even though exhaustion sank me into Nathan's mattress. There was no way we could all sleep together in his queen-sized bed, but I tried to memorize every second of their touch, their presence.

"So, what now?" Charlotte asked, and my worn-out ass and brain didn't allow me to do anything but exhale.

"Liam?" Nathan questioned.

"Hmm?" I couldn't even open my eyes.

"This was your idea, so I'm guessing you thought it all out well and good."

"Mmm hmm."

"So how do we do this?" Nathan asked. "I've got a million and one fantasies about the three of us fucking, but what about daily living? I've got a kid for fuck's sake. Can't just slam one of you against the wall and take you no matter how much I want it."

Char shivered between us as my sore ass clenched.

"We date each other," I said, forcing my brain to wake up a bit by cracking open an eyelids.

Nathan's dark ones peered at me from the other pillow, Char's crown of hair between us.

"If I'm working, I expect you to spoil our girl," I told him.

"Yes, please," Charlotte mumbled from between us.

"If she's working," I said with a sassy grin, "I expect the same."

His beard twitched. "My needy little lovers."

"Little." Charlotte snorted.

I pinched her thigh. "You're a lush peach, Char, and I love you just the way you are."

"Same," Nathan grunted. "Always have."

"Same," I whispered, finally working my hand between their bodies to rest my palm on her soft belly.

She pressed her cheek against Nathan's chest, and I leaned in, brushing my lips over his.

"Love your stubborn, reluctant ass too," I told him.

His eyes hooded as he gripped my backside hard enough I gasped. "You just love when I wreck your hole and make you cry."

"That's true too," I whispered with a tone that suggested I wanted his dick again even though my body couldn't handle it.

He chuckled and closed his eyes. "You both own me."

Finally. Fucking *finally*.

NATHAN DIDN'T WANT issues that would come in the morning with Trina if we spent the night, so Charlotte and I went home. I showed up again after ten the next morning with his permission, a box of donuts in one hand and my nail polish collection boxed up in the other.

"Where's the little pumpkin?" I asked, setting my stuff on the kitchen table.

"Playing in her room."

My bear had been out splitting wood, I swore it was all he ever did, and had followed me inside. His heat pressed against my back, the scent of his sweat filling my nose. Dick in a semi-hardened state, I pushed my ass against his groin with a throaty moan.

"You can't tease me like that and not promise fulfillment."

"Later," he whispered harshly in my ear, grabbing my ass and squeezing to the point I squeaked.

"Hi-ya!" Trina sing-songed while dancing toward us from the hallway, Lambey cuddled close.

"Hi." I held up my bag as Nathan's heat disappeared. "Look what I brought."

"What?" She climbed up onto a chair, and I popped open the plastic lid of my polish organizer. "Ooo!" Eyes like saucers, she dug in, rifling through colors, naming them one by one. Every time a sparkly hue caught her attention, she added a squeal.

I picked up my favorite matte black, the one I went to when feeling goth. "Whatcha think?" I asked her.

Nose wrinkling, she shook her head. "I hate black."

"You know what *I* hate?" I put the polish back in with the rest. "Bees. They scare me."

"I *hate* bees."

Hell, this little kid could own my heart. I smiled, angling another chair to sit beside her. "So what's it going to be?" I asked. "Pink? Purple?"

"Gween with spawkles for this one." She pointed at her pinky. "Wed and blue for this." Index and middle. "Yellow hewe, and owange for my thumb." Trina set out the colors in order, tickling my OCD nature and widening my grin.

"And what about your other hand?"

"Hmm. Let's see…" She took her time rifling through the rest of my collection, pulling some out and changing her mind a half-dozen or so times. She eventually settled on five different shades of pink—for Charlotte, the pig in her favorite book.

"You got it, pumpkin."

"Toes, too?" Big blue eyes delivered a puppy dog look no man could deny.

Two more lines of five ended up atop the table,

minus black, and I chuckled, glancing over at my man.

Nathan leaned against the counter, sucking down a glass of ice water, his gaze soft on the two of us. "What's the hospital think of you having nail polish on at work?"

"I don't wear it to work. It's a stay-at-home thing."

"You can wear it here. That strawberry-flavored lip gloss too."

"Like that, do you?" I asked with a smirk.

He adjusted the bulge in his jeans and licked his lower lip with a wink.

Yeah. He liked it, alright.

Dick officially hard, I turned my focus on Trina, determined to make her a friend for life. Being in Nathan's for good meant she would eventually be mine too. What better way to bond than over painting nails?

And with her precise order of polishes all facing the same way in perfectly spaced lines?

"I think we're going to be the best of friends, pumpkin," I told her.

"You alweady my new best fwiend," she stated, and that was that.

"I'm in," I tossed over my shoulder at Nathan.

"Never had a doubt." He left us alone to split more wood.

His fine ass hugged in denim gave me an eyeful and mind full of things to think on while trying to keep a four-year-old still in order for me to paint twenty, tiny fingernails and toes.

34

NATHAN

Agatha agreed to babysit Trina, and the three of us went out on our first real date the following night. We sat on a semi-circle booth in the back of the Italian restaurant in downtown Rawlings, Charlotte in between us, right where she belonged.

While I wondered about her comfort level, I didn't doubt Liam's. He'd been out and proud for years and had nothing to lose, no face to save. The hospital had hired a unicorn, glitter-loving gay man who didn't give a shit what other people thought, but Char and I were a different story.

Char had grown up in our shithole town where everyone knew everyone, and her pink cheeks and downturned gaze screamed of embarrassment over being squished between two men in our booth.

My scowl had been firmly embedded on my face when she and I had shown up at Liam's place, and I realized it remained even after we ordered our pizza.

"What's on your mind, big boy?" Liam asked, folding his arms and leaning onto the table to better see me on the other side of Charlotte.

Char glanced up at me as though she'd noted my aggravation too.

"Agatha is going to talk."

"And?" Liam questioned.

"The whole town will be gossiping before morning."

"And?" He repeated, his tone letting me know he didn't give a shit just like I'd expected. "Fuck whoever gets their panties in a twist," he said when I didn't expand on what bothered me. "They're just jealous bitches."

I glanced down at Char. "I don't want you catching any shit for being involved with two men."

"Like I said, jealous bitches," Liam murmured.

"Always the protective one." Char cupped my cheek, the love in her eyes easing the furrow in my brow a little. "It never fails to make my girly bits all tingly."

I wanted to tell her other ways I could make her girly bits tingle, but the waitress arrived with our drinks, and I sat back, taking note of Liam's goofy grin flatline fast as fuck.

His focus ensnared on tapping his straw on the table to break through the paper wrapper.

"What's wrong?" Charlotte asked before I could demand an answer over his sudden demeanor change.

"Billy Jenkins," Liam said at the same time I turned to find the man sitting down at the bar behind me.

"I thought you two had a truce of sorts," I said, eyeing the bully and his "kill the fag" crew who hadn't seemed to notice us.

"It's more the assholes with him I'm worried about," Liam muttered. He slunk down a bit on the bench, probably in an attempt to hide. He picked at the straw's paper, folding it in half and in half again.

Charlotte grasped his hand to still the nervous twitch.

My scowl returned full force at seeing him beaten down so easily. "I won't let them touch you."

"I know."

"And if one of them so much as breathes in your direction," I kept my voice low, the threat very real, "I'll smash their face in so fucking bad they'll need your skills in order to fix their ugly mug."

Holding my gaze, he wrapped his lips around his straw, and in the moment, I knew my going all "alpha growly" made him hard.

I zoned in on his mouth, and he sucked down some soda, exaggerating the licking of his lip—and the straw's tip once done. "You're a little tease," I grumbled.

"And you love it."

A full-on smirk would only encourage him, but I couldn't stop it from twitching my whiskers. "I do."

"Is he getting hard, Char?" Liam asked while watching me intently.

"Liam," she chided quietly.

"Check for me."

With a tiny huff, her arm shifted beneath the table, and my jaw clenched at her gentle grasp. Swelling of my groin took over.

"He is," Char whispered, and sure enough, pink fused her cheeks.

"You're stunning when embarrassed," Liam whispered, trailing his fingertip over her cheek, and I grunted my agreement.

"Thanks." She glanced away, pulling her hands back to her own lap, lacing her fingers together. The flush deepened to blotch down over her chest and the cleavage she left on full display.

She'd become a tease too after having a second taste of my cock.

"You look good enough to eat, Char," Liam told her. "Doesn't she, Nathan? All that creamy, soft skin. Red lips, hair in waves just begging for your fist."

"Liam."

His pupils swelled at my low tone which was full of lust and the promise of a heavy hand if he didn't behave in public.

"What?" He widened his not-so-innocent gaze while sitting back. "Don't tell me you haven't dreamed about her riding me, sliding your dick in alongside mine and holding onto that long mane to keep your soul grounded here on earth as heaven called out your name."

Charlotte let out a soft whimper, her backside antsy on the booth, and I rubbed a hand down over my beard.

Liam shifted as though his asshole clenched over my stare. "Think you can take us both, sweet Char?" he whispered, tearing his focus off me. Those eyes he'd been giving stated he wanted to climb over the table and beg me to stretch his hole so fast and hard he felt me in the back of his throat.

"I-I don't know?" The shade on her face turned more red than pink.

The waitress breezed in with steaming pizzas, and I sat back, the silence around our table tense and heavy. "Enjoy!" she said, flouncing away.

Oh, we definitely will.

"I'd like to try," Char whispered the second the woman moved out of ear shot.

My balls ached. To be inside Charlotte, my dick rubbing against Liam's... *Fuck yeah.*

Liam adjusted himself again, letting out a soft groan, and a shiver pebbled the skin on Char's arms.

"My needy little lovers," I chuckled, reaching for a slice of cheese pizza.

"Don't tell me the thought of being shoved inside her with me doesn't make you rock hard," Liam shot back, as though suddenly failing to see the humor because they both wanted a bed and privacy stat.

"I am *rock* hard." I tore into the pizza, and he gulped, his hand shaking while grabbing his own slice. More like granite, but my dick could wait. It wasn't like I could get them home to my place and fuck them the second Agatha left. Trina still had a few hours until bedtime. She was my pumpkin, but selfishness sometimes reared in a man's mind.

As for moving forward with our relationship, I thought I'd gone all in, headfirst and eyes wide open, but it only took an inquisitive Agatha upon asking her to babysit to get me up in arms and put me in a funk.

I'd told her I had a date with Charlotte but found myself hesitating over mentioning Liam in the equation. Why hesitate if I didn't give a shit what people thought about the three of us being together?

Because Char would catch shit, I had no doubt. Being with two men? And even if Liam did have it right about gossipers just being jealous bitches, I didn't want her—or him—to be looked down on. Picked on. Teased.

The thought burned my gut to the point I wanted to smash something. Maybe after my date, I'd head out to the woodpile for another date with my axe.

Charlotte squeezed my thigh beneath the table, her simple touch calming me. "Are you okay?"

"Yeah." I grabbed another piece of pizza and forced the skin on my forehead to smooth the fuck out. Time to change the fucking topic. "Agatha told me she heard you got your student assignments for the fall."

"Twenty-four kids, all but three of them boys."

"Oh, shit." Liam chuckled.

"Poopy," Char quietly chided.

"They're going to run your ass ragged," Liam continued, ignoring her correction.

"She'll have us to pamper her," I reminded them both, hoping for a future I desperately wanted to come easy but expected wouldn't.

"Fuck." Liam paled, and I twisted to see what he quickly glanced away from.

Billy Jenkins approached our table, hands shoved in his pockets. He cleared his throat, stopping a good three feet away from us, his gaze turning wary and shoulders tensing as our gazes clashed. "Nathan."

"Billy." Figured I'd acknowledge him like an adult since his stance didn't scream aggression.

"Liam tell you what he did for my woman?"

"If you mean saved her life when he could have walked away after all the shit you pulled when we were younger, yeah."

"Nathan," Char hissed, but I kept my glare on the asshole who'd blackened my boyfriend's eyes more times than I could count.

Billy's gaze flitted between me and Liam. "Rumor going around town about you two guys kissing in your garage."

Guys, not fags, but still.

I narrowed my gaze, my insides tight, fists ready to roll if necessary. "What of it?"

Charlotte clutched at my thigh as though she thought I'd hop up and rearrange Billy's face. She had it right if he pushed.

Billy shrugged. "Just wanted to let you know Liam here's a good man and I wish you both the best."

Well, fuck me sideways.

If the leader of the "kill the fag" crew was willing to accept it...

Time to own the fact I'd stand up to anyone thinking to hurt what belonged to me. That I wanted what and *who* I wanted, fuck what all others considered right or wrong.

"Gonna have to include Charlotte in those best wishes," I told Billy, lifting my chin. "Because she's mine too."

A glint lit in his eye as he glanced at her but one I never in a million years would have expected considering his years of tormenting her—jealousy. "You're a lucky bastard, Nathan."

I slung an arm around Char's shoulders and grabbed hold of Liam's shirt beyond her, tugging them both in tight. "Damn right."

"Thanks again, Liam." Billy stuck his hand out, and Liam accepted his offer. "We're lucky to have you here. You're a damn good surgeon."

The three of us stared as Billy sauntered back to his barstool.

"Well," Charlotte breathed, letting out a soft giggle. "If the town bully gives his approval, I think we're golden."

I kissed the top of her head.

"And with that," Liam said, tossing a hundred-dollar bill onto the table, "it's time to celebrate."

"Where are we going?" Charlotte asked.

"My place."

"Do you have ice cream and cherries for sundaes?"

"Nope," he said, sliding out of the booth, "but I have the biggest bed."

"Let's go." I pushed to stand, not even bothering with the leftover pizza. One hand swallowing Charlotte's, I helped her to her feet. I reached out the other to Liam, holding his gaze.

He grinned like Trina over chicken nuggies, and at the firm squeeze of his fingers against mine, any last bit of hesitation wanting to hang on slid away.

We caught a few stares, but I didn't give a shit. I had my lovers' backs.

Billy Jenkins lifted his beer toward us as we walked past, the three of us hand-in-hand, and while two of the three in his crew glanced our way with curled lips, I couldn't find a single fuck to give.

I was man enough to own what I wanted. Why I'd been reluctant in the first place beat the hell out of me. I loved two people, needed two people beside me and in my bed for the rest of my life.

It didn't matter what other people thought as long as we were together and happy.

And I had plans to make them happy.

Very fucking happy.

CHARLOTTE

"I imagined you here in my kitchen pulling out pans of freshly baked cookies," Liam told me while tossing his keys onto the kitchen island.

My face heated, my heart swelling at the thought we'd shared our imaginings.

"What else have you fantasized happening in this house?" Nathan asked while kicking off his boots.

Liam glanced down over my sundress. "I imagined watching you behind my shower's glass door, water running down around your gorgeous curves."

Oh goodness. "After?" I whispered, hoping my men wouldn't make me wait. The thought of taking the two of them at the same time scared the living daylights out of me, but I wanted it. Desperately, and not after showering first. I'd had enough teasing and was ready to try.

Liam held out his hand. "After."

Nathan grunted an agreement as I took his hand, and we turned, heading up the stairs to Liam's bedroom where we would spend the night.

Nathan had called Agatha on the way to Liam's place, asking if Trina could have a sleepover at her house. He told us after hanging up that Agatha had agreed as long as he promised to have fun and give her all the juicy details later.

He promised to, but I knew he wouldn't. Our lumberjack didn't share when it came to Liam and me.

My insides tightened to the point I wished I hadn't eaten a second slice of pizza, but Liam's soft mouth on mine and Nathan's hard warmth wrapping around me from behind calmed my racing mind. I didn't doubt we'd been fated for one another. I didn't doubt either of their love, their desire for me. And I wanted nothing more than to please the two men who'd brought so much bliss into my life.

Liam stripped and lay down, his glasses set aside, his blue eyes nearly overtaken by black pupils. "Come here, Char. Let me taste you."

My core clenched at his words. Nathan's large

hands slid over over my waist, slipping my sundress to the floor. "H-how?" I asked, eyeing Liam laid back on the bed.

"Straddle his face," Nathan whispered hotly against my ear.

Sit on his face. I almost snorted at the thought, but the heat in Liam's eyes and the rumble of Nathan's voice sent me forward, stepping out of my dress and climbing onto the bed. My breasts swung as I moved over a man's body smaller than my own, but any embarrassment dissipated at Nathan's deep groan behind us.

"Fuck, that ass, Char. So fucking gorgeous."

Feeling like the sexiest thing on God's green earth, I slid over Liam's chest, rising onto my knees.

"Bring that pussy up here," he said, grasping my thighs and tugging me higher. "Right on my mouth."

Heat rushed through me, and I bit my lip to keep from whimpering.

Thick thighs bracketed Liam's face—and he lifted to meet me as I lowered, his tongue delving right into my core.

"Oh!" I grabbed hold of his headboard, eyes clenching shut, and fought the need to ride his face like a cowgirl as he lapped and suckled on every bit of my flesh.

He grunted, his fingers tightening on my thighs, and I glanced behind to find Nathan had taken his dick into his mouth.

"Fuck," Liam muttered against my lower lips, and he swiped through my folds, moaning and whimpering enough for the both of us.

So hot—so fucking hot.

"Nathan," Liam groaned, and I lifted enough to let him breathe. "Fuck, man, you've got to stop." Liam panted beneath me, and I shivered atop him, as ready as he was.

"Just getting you good and slick for our woman," Nathan said, his voice tight, wet sounds pulling my attention over my shoulder again. Saliva and precum smeared down Liam's erection beneath Nathan's palm, and he worked his own length with his other hand.

My core fluttered, and I licked my lip, knowing the wetness of my arousal would be more than enough to ease their way.

"Sit on his dick, Char."

I scooted back at Nathan's command, keeping on hands and knees, but Nathan grabbed my backside before I could sink down onto the length Liam held straight up for me.

Nathan spread my cheeks, letting out another

curse. "This ass…" He licked up over my entire backside, his tongue running lightly over my puckered hole. "Someday, Char. Some day."

I clenched at his word, holding Liam's gaze as he offered a lazy smirk.

"You'll like it," he said with a saucy wink. "Trust me."

Nathan grasped my hips and lowered me onto Liam's waiting dick, and quiet moans left us both as I settled fully on his length.

"Make yourself good and wet, Char, because I want in there too."

I moved at Nathan's instruction, shifting forward and backward, rubbing my clit along Liam's hard abs. Lips parted, we stared at one another, the rush of my blood in my ears, the passion in his eyes filling my heart up.

Nathan moved in my periphery, tearing my focus off Liam.

He retrieved a small bottle of lube from the bed stand and disappeared from view again.

"I love watching his dick stretch you," Nathan said from behind me, the wet sounds of him slickening his length as much of a turn on as his words. "Gonna take this pretty pink pussy too, Char. Stuff you full."

Panting, I dropped my head, eyes clenched shut and arms shaking as he dribbled coolness down over my backside. He lubed up every inch of me, even smearing it over my cheeks. He grasped Liam's length as I shifted forward, keeping two fingers in place as I sank back again, impaling myself.

A dick and two fingers...more than I'd ever taken, but staying relaxed kept it from burning too badly.

"Giving you another one," Nathan said after a few strokes, his hand on my hip guiding me forward and back.

"Okay," I whispered, letting out a steady exhale, a shiver rippling over me at the sting of being stretched too far.

Full. So damn full…

"Shit." Liam cursed again as though he clenched his jaw, but I couldn't open my eyes to check.

Tremors wracked through me, and my elbows threatened to collapse.

"Come here," Liam said, pulling me down atop him.

"Too heavy," I complained, but he took my mouth, shutting me up, turning off all thought but feeling. Emotion swelled in my chest, so much love and desire that my heart wanted to burst at the fullness. His hands smoothed down my back, his dick nudging into me as Nathan's fingers probed and stretched.

Too much stimulation. Too much, yet not enough.

"Please," I whispered against Liam's mouth, my eyes welling, my throat tightening. "Nathan…"

His fingers disappeared, and something bigger, blunter, pressed against the back of Liam's length buried inside me. "Relax, Char. Let out a steady exhale and relax."

Liam held me close, and I buried my face in his neck. My inhale shuddered, but I leaked it out slowly, focusing on loosening my core, my muscles.

Nathan pushed, and I imagined my body opening up for him. Stinging pain rose, and I bit my lip to keep from crying out.

"That's it, Char. Fuck, that's it." He breached, and my breath left in a whimpered rush.

"Shh," Liam whispered, gathering up my hair and moving my mouth to his. Tender and so soft, he caressed my lips, his tongue licking, as soothing as Nathan's palms gliding over my slick backside, both of them remaining still, giving me time to adjust.

The burn from their combined girth eased, and I tore my mouth off Liam's. "I-I'm okay."

Nathan eased in a further, and I gasped a deep inhale, filling my lungs with Liam's spicy cologne.

"Tell me that feels good, Char," he said, his voice tight, "because I've never felt anything better. Nathan's dick against mine inside your hot pussy. Fuck."

A deep groan of agreement sounded from Nathan as his hairy thighs brushed along my backside. "Christ, Char…" He rocked his hips, sliding in deeper. "Holy fuck."

"Move," I whispered at Liam's ear, and he gave me what I needed.

More friction. Opposing motion, a constant ebb and flow.

A finger slid over my back entrance, and I let out a groan, relaxing even more. I wanted him there…

"Yes," I told him, and he pressed, the lube making for an easy glide through the ring of muscle wanting to keep his finger out.

Much too full. Overstimulated by too much, and yet never enough.

My toes tingled, my body tightening in readiness to climax. "More," I begged, moving back to meet their thrusts.

A hand fisted in my hair, yanking me back, and I

sat, my breasts jutting forward as a cry ripped from my lips.

"Goddamn, Char." Nathan's whiskers rubbed my throat, his teeth nipping along my flesh as he pumped his hips against me, filling me. With his finger still deep inside my body I felt filthy, dirty. "So fucking good taking our dicks like this. Wet and hot. So tight. Suck her tits, Liam."

Liam lifted onto an elbow, grabbed one of my swaying breasts, and covered my nipple with his mouth. Every pull of suction shot straight to my clit, and I cried out again, trying to shift my hips to get friction where I needed it as both men continued to thrust inside me.

"More. Please." I gasped, reaching back to grab hold of Nathan's head. "Please, Nathan. I…I need."

He sucked on my neck and pulled his finger from my backside. A quick rustle of sheets like he wiped his fingers clean and he reached around my belly, his slick fingers finding my clit. "This?" he asked, teasing me with gentle glides over my throbbing nub.

"Yes," I groaned and ground against his hand, chasing the rising climax. "More. Harder."

His hold on my hair tightened as he gave me what I needed, slamming deep inside me and jostling me in Liam's hold. Teeth scraped over my nipple, and Nathan pinched my clit.

I shrieked as my climax broke over me like an ocean's swell, drowning me in breath-stealing ecstasy, emptying my mind of anything but release. Core clenching, the rush of wetness and the tingling racing through my blood and over my skin consumed me.

Both men grunted, curses filled my ears, but their voices turned hazy as I floated down between them, hot, sweaty skin pressing against my front and back. Sandwiched between their hard bodies.

Cheese.

I huffed a giggle through my gasps for breath and closed my eyes.

36

LIAM

Nathan washed Charlotte in my shower while I stood outside the glass door, fulfilling one of my many fantasies. She'd felt like perfection cradling our dicks the way she had. I'd never experienced anything so amazing, so tight and hot in all my life.

She'd become my new addiction. The sounds leaving her lips as we'd taken her, given her what she begged for. I hadn't been able to move all that much, but the glide of Nathan's dick against mine...

I took myself in hand, my focus on the soapy water running along Char's curves and Nathan's huge paws mapping out every inch of her skin. His voice rumbled against her neck, her resulting smile like a lancing beam of light straight though my heart.

Crooked top teeth, plump cheeks, her dark eyes shining while watching me palm myself, Charlotte was beautiful heaven.

I let myself into my huge shower stall, needing to get my hands on her again.

She giggled as I pressed against her backside, once more squishing her between us.

"You're so soft and delicious," I said, placing a kiss on her shoulder. "I never imagined it would be this good."

"But you hoped?"

"From the moment I realized we could share you, yes." I met Nathan's gaze over her shoulder. Tenderness filled his eyes, the skin between his eyebrows smooth for a change. "What are you thinking, big boy?"

One corner of his lips curled upward, sending butterflies through me. "I'm thinking I wasted twenty years of my life."

"Don't. We all learned and lived. Gained experience and lessons we wouldn't have otherwise."

"I suppose you're right," he agreed as Charlotte settled her cheek on his chest, a satiated smile on her lips. "But we're going to have to make up for lost time."

"I might need a break here and there," she said

with a giggle. "Too much cheese isn't always a good thing."

Nathan barked out a laugh, and I grinned like a fool. "You'll have to take out your extra aggression on me," I told him, my ass tingling with anticipation.

"Can I watch?" Char asked.

"Fuck yeah," Nathan said, grabbing hold of my ass and pulling us tight against him.

"So I was thinking," I said, pushing Char's wet hair off her shoulder and to the side. "What would the two of you think about moving in here with me?"

"But you like quiet and privacy," she said with a sigh, without a trace of argument in her voice.

"Not when it comes to you two, I don't." I met Nathan's stare. "I have the biggest bed. The biggest house with the most bedrooms. I even have two extra—one for Trina, the other for Char's messy library I wouldn't ever ask her to leave behind."

"And when one of us puts a baby in her belly?"

My dick twitched back to life. "Then we rearrange," I stated, my voice raspy with desire to fulfill Char's dreams. "We adjust."

"Hopefully sooner than later." Char nuzzled Nathan's hairy chest.

"Pretty sure we'll be fucking every damn day for

the foreseeable future," he said, "but you tell us when it's time to try, Char, and I promise you we'll both drain ourselves dry attempting to give you what you've always wanted."

"What I want are little minis of both of you. They'll be the cherries on top of my life's sundae."

Chuckling, Nathan bent down to kiss her, and I closed my eyes, resting my cheek on the back of her head, their sighs, the sounds of their tongues and lips coming together just what my needy ass wanted in that moment.

Pure fucking bliss.

37

NATHAN

Trina stood in front of the kitchen chair I lounged in while I brushed her hair, her little head tipping to the side whenever I drew the teeth down through the silky, dark strands. We'd come a long way in our somewhat short time together since the summer had begun. She'd given me her trust from day one, and I, in turn, had handed over my heart long before the cooler weather had moved in, rattling the kitchen window.

At first, I'd been reluctant to take on what I'd seen as baggage.

How wrong I'd been.

She'd been the spark, the fuse my life needed. She'd lit up my world and given me a new outlook, but just as importantly, she'd brought me home to a place I never thought I'd set foot in again.

I'd come back a different man though. Like Liam had said, I'd learned some lessons. Learned what I did and didn't want, even if it took returning to the beginning in order for me to realize that truth.

Trina had become my new truth, Charlotte and Liam the cherry atop a sundae, as my woman would say. And while Liam and I had been trying to impregnate her for close to two weeks straight, I would have been content, happy with all I'd gained.

All due to my brother's death.

A man who'd left me behind, a ward of the state.

I never thought I'd forgive him for what he'd done, but I found myself less angry, the bitterness in me eased by what I'd found—because of him.

"Do you miss your daddy?" I asked, my tone gruffer than I'd meant or expected.

"You my daddy now," Trina didn't hesitate to answer, and I dropped the brush onto the table, pulling her up into my arms, my eyes stinging.

"And you're my little pumpkin."

She clutched at my neck, giggling while rubbing her face in my whiskers. "Tickley."

"Lambey likes my whiskers."

"Nuh uh."

I swallowed against the tightness in my throat even though I grinned. Pulling back, I studied her big blue eyes. "What would you think about having another daddy?"

Tears welled, and I realized I'd fucked up.

"Awe you leaving me?"

"No! No, pumpkin," I hurried to say, tugging on her soft hair. "I meant having two daddies."

She studied me, her little lips pursed. "My fwiend who paints my nails?" She wiggled her hand in front of my face, showing off the new red, yellow, and purple manicure Liam had given her the day before.

"Yeah," I said, my heart aching. "Your friend who paints your fingernails and piggy toes."

"Okay. I like him."

"And what about a mommy?"

Her eyes widened, her smile hitting me like an axe to the chest. "Chawlotte who makes the *best* chocolate chip cookies?"

"That would be the one."

"Then yes, please!" She wiggled, and I set her down. Her socked feet slapped on the linoleum and hardwood as she sprinted back through the hallway. "Lambey! We getting a mommy and a new daddy too!"

A laugh tore from my lips, one I bit back since

my damn eyes hazed over with tears. That had gone ten times easier than I'd expected, and I couldn't be more pleased with the outcome.

Wiping the back of my hand over my eyes, I pulled my cell from my back pocket.

I had two phone calls to make.

What sucked is I couldn't decide who to call first.

38

TRINA

THREE YEARS LATER

"Ready?" Daddy squatted down in front of me, his dark eyes happier than I'd ever seen.

"How loud are we talking?" I asked, raising an eyebrow.

"Sassy squirt." He ruffled my hair, and I shied away, smoothing down the French braids Agatha had done for me earlier that morning. "They can get loud, but I'll bet you work your magic like you did on Lambey when she got grumpy."

"Pah-lease." I rolled my eyes even though my heart still warmed whenever I thought of my favorite stuffy who still sat in the VIP section atop my pillow sham.

"Come on." Daddy stood and held out his hand.

While I'd grown up—too much for my britches, he claimed—nervousness fluttered my belly. I held his hand, and the butterflies faded like they always did when he squeezed me tight.

I took a deep breath and stuck close as he pushed into the hospital room.

Something smelled like shit, but I didn't say it out loud since Mom would "chide" as Daddy would say.

Daddy Liam sat in a rocking chair beside Mom's bed, a little bundle wrapped in pink in his arms.

I stared, my eyes probably super wide, my free hand wiping down my jeans.

A squawk pulled my focus off my baby sister to the squirming thing in Mom's arms. My baby brother, the one Daddy had said liked to scream a lot. Another squawk and Mom laughed, rubbing his face all over her boob.

He shut up quick, and Daddy put his hand on my back. "Go on."

I went to Daddy Liam first since the baby he held wasn't squirming or squealing. She had a tiny face, the cutest little nose I'd ever seen, and eyes as clear blue as the sky. "She looks just like you," I said, lifting my head to find his eyes all wet like he wanted to cry or something.

"Yeah." Daddy Liam only spoke one word, getting all quiet again.

Grinning, I glanced down at my baby sister again, crowding in close to touch her pink cheek. "She's so damn cute!"

"Trina."

"Sorry, Mom," I said automatically over my cursing without lifting my head. "When can I hold her?"

"Whenever you want," Daddy Liam said, his voice shaky.

"You're pretty happy, huh?" I grinned at him.

"Yeah, pumpkin. I am."

I looked over to see Daddy had sat on Mom's hospital bed, his face doing the same funny thing like Daddy Liam's.

"Guess I'll go see the squawker."

Daddy Liam chuckled at my whisper, and I stepped over to see the dark-haired loud one drinking milk from Mom's boob.

"Daddy said he shuts up after he eats," I muttered, not so sure I was going to like the squirmy baby.

"Usually, yes," Mom said, her fingertips trying to get the mess of hair atop my brother's hair to slick down.

Unlike my sister, he lay on Mom in just a diaper,

his skin darker like Daddy's, like he spent all day out cutting down trees and splitting wood.

"What color are his eyes?" I asked since his face all but smooshed into Mom's softness.

"Brown like his daddy's."

Daddy grinned, and the happiness I saw on his face made me smile too.

"Can I hold him?" I asked, deciding that my baby brother must not be too bad if Daddy liked him.

"Sure thing, sweet girl."

"What's his name?" I asked, touching his tiny toes until they wiggled.

"We haven't named him yet," Daddy said. "Figured we would wait until you got here so we could all decide together what to call them."

I'd been scared when I first found out Mom was going to have babies. I got even more scared when we found out she had twins in her huge belly. Two more kids in our house, two kids they might love more than me since I didn't belong to them.

Not really.

I listened in a few times when they talked about things not meant for kids. I knew they'd spent a lot of money to put those babies in Mom's belly.

A lot.

"Come here, pumpkin." Daddy pulled me up onto

his lap and rested his chin on the top of my head once I settled where I could still see my baby brother and sister. "I love you more than anything. You know that, right?"

My throat swelled up tight like I wanted to cry, so I nodded instead of answering.

"You've been in my heart since the first time I saw you three years ago. And these two? They're just there with you now. They'll never take your special place inside me, okay?"

"O-okay," I squeaked out along with a tear.

Two minutes later, I sat on the rocking chair, one blue-eyed baby in one arm, one dark-eyed baby in the other. "They don't look anything alike," I said, frowning while looking at one then the other and back again.

"It's because they have two different daddies," Mom said.

"Oh." I didn't understand, but the boy farted really loud, and the sudden stink gagged me.

"He shit himself!" I gagged, trying to turn my face as far away from him as possible.

"Poopy," Mom said with a sigh.

She hated when I cussed like Daddy, but some-times it just came out—like my little brother's *poopy.*

"Take him," I said, gasping over my shoulder for fresh air.

Daddy laughed and lifted his son, holding him away from his body. "Holy hell, he stinks."

"*Told* you." I snuggled my sister closer, lifting her forehead to my nose. "Now *you* smell good. Like powder and Mom."

Daddy Liam tugged on my braid from where he squatted beside me.

"You love her pretty much, huh?" I asked him.

"No more than I love you."

My throat got all tight again. "I love you too, Daddy Liam."

He leaned up and kissed my cheek before leaving me alone to check on Mom.

"We're going to be the bestest of friends," I whispered to my sister, "but that other one, the stinky boy, can hang out with us too, I guess. You're going to share a room until you're older, but some day, you're going to move into my room. We'll have bunkbeds and everything. Oh, and *wait* until you have real teeth and Daddy makes us French toast. You're going to *love* it."

THE END

. . .

IF YOU ENJOYED RELUCTANT LUMBERJACK, **please leave a review! Just a line or two offering your honest opinion would be deeply appreciated.**

If you enjoyed this MMF romance, be sure to check out my other poly pairings on my website.

ABOUT THE AUTHOR

Spicy romance author Lynn Burke believes everyone deserves healing and a happily ever after. She loves writing hot, inclusive stories of various pairings or triplings and creates characters who will steal your heart.

She is a USA Today Bestselling author, a wrangler of her three spawn, and a farmer's daughter who grows organic food. To escape reality, she hides in a quiet corner with her nose in a book.

You can find more about Lynn at her website: www.authorlynnburke.com

Pippen Creek Series

Risso Family Series

Sandy Ridge Series

Sinful Nature Series

Vicious Vipers MC